Make Him Pay

Karma Series, Volume 2

Lexy Timms

Published by Wanita May, 2021.

This is a work of fiction. Similarities to real people, places, or events are entirely coincidental.

MAKE HIM PAY

First edition. March 1, 2021.

Copyright © 2021 Lexy Timms.

Written by Lexy Timms.

Also by Lexy Timms

A Bad Boy Bullied Romance
I Hate You
I Hate You A Little Bit
I Hate You A Little Bit More

A Burning Love Series
Spark of Passion
Flame of Desire
Blaze of Ecstasy

A Chance at Forever Series
Forever Perfect
Forever Desired
Forever Together

A Dating App Series
I've Been Matched
You've Been Matched

We've Been Matched

A "Kind of" Billionaire
Taking a Risk
Safety in Numbers
Pretend You're Mine

A Maybe Series
Maybe I Should
Maybe I Shouldn't
Maybe I Did

Assisting the Boss Series
Billion Reasons
Duke of Delegation
Late Night Meetings
Delegating Love
Suitors and Admirers

BBW Romance Series
Capturing Her Beauty
Pursuing Her Dreams
Tracing Her Curves

Beating the Biker Series

Making Her His
Making the Break
Making of Them

Betrayal at the Bay Series
Devil's Bay
Devil's Deceit

Billionaire Banker Series
Banking on Him
Price of Passion
Investing in Love
Knowing Your Worth
Treasured Forever
Banking on Christmas
Billionaire Banker Box Set Books #1-3

Billionaire CEO Brothers
Tempting the Player
Late Night Boardroom
Reviewing the Perfomance
Result of Passion
Directing the Next Move
Touching the Assets

Billionaire Holiday Romance Series

Driving Home for Christmas
The Valentine Getaway
Cruising Love
Billionaire Holiday Romance Box Set

Billionaire in Disguise Series
Facade
Illusion
Charade

Billionaire Secrets Series
The Secret
Freedom
Courage
Trust
Impulse
Billionaire Secrets Box Set Books #1-3

Blind Sight Series
See Me
Fix Me
Eyes On Me

Branded Series
Money or Nothing
What People Say

Her Personal Assistant - Part 2
Her Personal Assistant Box Set

Fake Billionaire Series
Faking It
Temporary CEO
Caught in the Act
Never Tell A Lie
Fake Christmas
Fake Billionaire Box Set #1-3

Firehouse Romance Series
Caught in Flames
Burning With Desire
Craving the Heat
Firehouse Romance Complete Collection

Forging Billions Series
Dirty Money
Petty Cash
Payment Required

For His Pleasure
Elizabeth
Georgia
Madison

Fortune Riders MC Series
Billionaire Biker
Billionaire Ransom
Billionaire Misery
Fortune Riders Box Set - Books #1-3

Fragile Series
Fragile Touch
Fragile Kiss
Fragile Love

Great Temptation Series
The Devil's Footsteps
Heaven's Command
Mortals Surrender

Hades' Spawn Motorcycle Club
One You Can't Forget
One That Got Away
One That Came Back
One You Never Leave
One Christmas Night
Hades' Spawn MC Complete Series

Hard Rocked Series
Rhyme
Harmony
Lyrics

Heart of Stone Series
The Protector
The Guardian
The Warrior

Heart of the Battle Series
Celtic Viking
Celtic Rune
Celtic Mann
Heart of the Battle Series Box Set

Heistdom Series
Master Thief
Goldmine
Diamond Heist
Smile For Me
Your Move
Green With Envy
Saving Money

Highlander Wolf Series
Pack Run
Pack Land
Pack Rules

Hollyweird Fae Series
Inception of Gold
Disruption of Magic
Guardians of Twilight

How To Love A Spy
The Secret
The Secret Life
The Secret Wife

Just About Series
About Love
About Truth
About Forever
Just About Box Set Books #1-3

Justice Series
Seeking Justice
Finding Justice

Chasing Justice
Pursuing Justice
Justice - Complete Series

Karma Series
Walk Away
Make Him Pay

Kissed by Billions
Kissed by Passion
Kissed by Desire
Kissed by Love

Leaning Towards Trouble
Trouble
Discord
Tenacity

Love on the Sea Series
Ships Ahoy
Rough Sea
High Tide

Love You Series
Love Life

Need Love
My Love

Managing the Billionaire
Never Enough
Worth the Cost
Secret Admirers
Chasing Affection
Pressing Romance
Timeless Memories
Managing the Billionaire Box Set Books #1-3

Managing the Bosses Series
The Boss
The Boss Too
Who's the Boss Now
Love the Boss
I Do the Boss
Wife to the Boss
Employed by the Boss
Brother to the Boss
Senior Advisor to the Boss
Forever the Boss
Christmas With the Boss
Billionaire in Control
Billionaire Makes Millions
Billionaire at Work
Precious Little Thing
Priceless Love
Valentine Love

Crossing the Bluff
Climbing the Mount

My Best Friend's Sister
Hometown Calling
A Perfect Moment
Thrown in Together

My Darker Side Series
Darkest Hour
Time to Stop
Against the Light

Neverending Dream Series
Neverending Dream - Part 1
Neverending Dream - Part 2
Neverending Dream - Part 3
Neverending Dream - Part 4
Neverending Dream - Part 5

Outside the Octagon
Submit
Fight
Knockout

Protecting Diana Series
Her Bodyguard
Her Defender
Her Champion
Her Protector
Her Forever

Protecting Layla Series
His Mission
His Objective
His Devotion

Racing Hearts Series
Rush
Pace
Fast

Regency Romance Series
The Duchess Scandal - Part 1
The Duchess Scandal - Part 2

Reverse Harem Series
Primals
Archaic

Unitary

RIP Series
Track the Ripper
Hunt the Ripper
Pursue the Ripper

R&S Rich and Single Series
Alex Reid
Parker
Sebastian

Saving Forever
Saving Forever - Part 1
Saving Forever - Part 2
Saving Forever - Part 3
Saving Forever - Part 4
Saving Forever - Part 5
Saving Forever - Part 6
Saving Forever Part 7
Saving Forever - Part 8
Saving Forever Boxset Books #1-3

Secrets & Lies Series
Strange Secrets
Evading Secrets

Inspiring Secrets
Lies and Secrets
Mastering Secrets
Alluring Secrets
Secrets & Lies Box Set Books #1-3

Shifting Desires Series
Jungle Heat
Jungle Fever
Jungle Blaze

Sin Series
Payment for Sin
Atonement Within
Declaration of Love

Southern Romance Series
Little Love Affair
Siege of the Heart
Freedom Forever
Soldier's Fortune

Spanked Series
Passion
Playmate
Pleasure

Spelling Love Series
The Author
The Book Boyfriend
The Words of Love

Taboo Wedding Series
He Loves Me Not
With This Ring
Happily Ever After

Tattooist Series
Confession of a Tattooist
Surrender of a Tattooist
Heart of a Tattooist
Hopes & Dreams of a Tattooist

Tennessee Romance
Whisky Lullaby
Whisky Melody
Whisky Harmony

The Bad Boy Alpha Club
Battle Lines - Part 1
Battle Lines

The Brush Of Love Series
Every Night
Every Day
Every Time
Every Way
Every Touch
The Brush of Love Series Box Set Books #1-3

The Debt
The Debt: Part 1 - Damn Horse
The Debt: Complete Collection

The Fire Inside Series
Dare Me
Defy Me
Burn Me

The Gentleman's Club Series
Gambler
Player
Wager

The Golden Mail
Hot Off the Press

Extra! Extra!
Read All About It
Stop the Press
Breaking News
This Just In
The Golden Mail Box Set Books #1-3

The Lucky Billionaire Series
Lucky Break
Streak of Luck
Lucky in Love

The Sound of Breaking Hearts Series
Disruption
Destroy
Devoted

The University of Gatica Series
The Recruiting Trip
Faster
Higher
Stronger
Dominate
No Rush
University of Gatica - The Complete Series

T.N.T. Series
Troubled Nate Thomas - Part 1
Troubled Nate Thomas - Part 2
Troubled Nate Thomas - Part 3

Toxic Touch Series
Noxious
Lethal
Willful
Tainted
Craved

Undercover Series
Perfect For Me
Perfect For You
Perfect For Us

Unknown Identity Series
Unknown
Unpublished
Unexposed
Unsure
Unwritten
Unknown Identity Box Set: Books #1-3

Standalone
Wash
Loving Charity
Summer Lovin'
Love & College
Billionaire Heart
First Love
Frisky and Fun Romance Box Collection
Beating Hades' Bikers
Everyone Loves a Bad Boy

Watch for more at www.lexytimms.com.

By LEXY TIMMS
Copyright 2021

Karma Series

Walk Away
Make Him Pay
Perfect Revenge

Find Lexy Timms:

LEXY TIMMS NEWSLETTER:
http://eepurl.com/9i0vD
Lexy Timms Facebook Page:
https://www.facebook.com/SavingForever
Lexy Timms Website:
http://www.lexytimms.com

Want to read more...
For **FREE**?
Sign up for Lexy Timms' newsletter
And she'll send you updates on new releases, ARC copies of books
and a whole lotta fun!
Sign up for news and updates!
http://eepurl.com/9i0vD

Make Him Pay

THE WORST THING ABOUT being lied to is knowing you weren't worth the truth...

Tatum Banks is on a mission to get revenge on her ex. By hooking up with her sexy best friend, Cooper Dunn she thinks she's found the perfect retaliation.

Except, the mission goes awry when she falls in love with the one man in her life that has always been there for her.

Cooper is tired of the revenge game and wants Tatum to let things go and just focus on their relationship. However, Tatum has one last objective. She found out her ex is stealing the work of authors and slapping his name on it. She decides it is her responsibility to expose the truth only to get dragged into a dangerous world of theft and cover-ups that could cost her everything.

I hated him so much because I had loved him too much.

Chapter One

Tatum

MY PALMS WERE SWEATY, and my stomach was a ball of nerves. Nothing felt right. I was certain I was going to puke at any second. Everything felt wrong. I couldn't lose him. I looked out the back window of the Uber. I didn't see him. That was a good thing. If he wasn't behind us, that meant he was staying at my apartment.

"Please stay." I breathed the words.

I couldn't believe I had walked out on the man I loved. I loved Cooper. I did. He had to know that. This thing with my ex, Austin, wasn't about him. It was about righting a horrible wrong. I wished I could make Cooper understand why this was so important to me.

Could I blame him for the ultimatum? No. No, I couldn't. I looked out the back window again. I didn't want to see his headlights. If I saw his headlights, it meant he'd left my apartment. If he left, we were over. I felt like we'd been walking a tightrope with no safety net for days. Longer. He thought I was hung up on my ex. I wasn't. This wasn't about my ex. It was about doing the right thing.

"You okay, miss?" the driver asked from up front.

"I'm fine."

"You were muttering."

"Yes, I was," I snapped. "I talk to myself."

"All right."

I stared out the window, asking myself over and over if I was doing the right thing. I loved Cooper. I wanted him. He was the only one I wanted. When he told me to choose between him and going to the party to confront Austin and my boss about their part in stealing the work of authors who didn't have the benefit of a publishing house in their corner, I had to go with my conscience.

I read that writer's blog. She was upset that her work was being published under another name. Some stranger was taking credit for her work and reaping the benefits. She got a tiny portion of the proceeds from what her book could have earned had she gotten her foot in the door and had an agent. It wasn't fair. It wasn't right, and I could not be complicit in their scheme.

I pulled out my phone to see if he'd called. I expected him to tell me to turn around. There was nothing. I sent him a quick text telling him I loved him and begging him to be waiting for me at my place. I was hoping to get to the party, get the information I needed on my handy little recorder, and get back to him.

The car pulled to a stop in front of the house. This was it. "Just a second," I said to the driver.

Cooper had yet to text me back. I called his phone. I needed to know he was waiting for me. He didn't answer. "Shit, shit, shit," I muttered.

I had never felt so twisted and torn. I knew what I wanted to do, but I couldn't just give up everything. "Um, sir," I said before I could change my mind.

"What's up?"

"I need to go back."

"Go back?"

"Yes, to the address you picked me up from." He let out a long sigh. "I'll make sure you're tipped well."

He pulled up his phone and after a few seconds, finally put the car in drive. "Fine. I can do that."

"Thank you." I tried calling Cooper again. He wasn't answering. This did not bode well for him being back at my place and waiting for me.

"Relationships are a bitch, huh?"

"I guess," I said and turned my attention back out the window.

I felt like I had just barely gotten started with Cooper. I loved him, but we had yet to have a solid relationship. It was like I went left when he went right. I supposed it was my fault. I was in this stupid holding pattern with Austin, and Cooper wasn't going to stand for it. I didn't blame him, but I wished he could just give me one more day. One day. Hell, one hour. Then he and I could have our moment of running off into the sunset together. Even if that meant staying right where we were.

"Don't leave," I told the driver when he pulled to a stop.

"What?"

"I'm going to need you to take me back to the original address."

"Are you kidding me?"

"No. It isn't like you aren't getting paid." He was irritating me. He got paid regardless of where I had him drive me to.

"I can't wait long," he answered. "I don't make money if I'm not driving."

"Got it."

I jumped out of the car and raced upstairs. I didn't have to, but I did it anyway. "Cooper!" His truck wasn't in the parking lot. I hoped against hope he would be here.

"Cooper!" I called out and walked to my bedroom. I flipped on the light and found the room was empty.

I fought back the tears. He was gone. I knew he would be, but I'd prayed he would wait. I took a deep breath and pushed back the tears. There was no point in crying. He was gone. I wanted him back, and I had every intention of fighting to get him back, but it was going to take a huge commitment. I didn't want to beg for his forgiveness just to walk out on him again. We'd been doing that same dance for weeks, and it wasn't working.

I needed to be prepared to go all in. I would give him my complete devotion. "Will it matter?"

I wished I could say there was a chance. Unfortunately, I didn't think my odds were very good. In fact, I was sure it would take a small miracle to get him to come back to me. If I was going to lose Cooper, it had to be for a damn good reason. I left the apartment and headed downstairs to the waiting car. I was going to a party, but it felt like I was going to a funeral.

"So we doing this?" the driver asked.

"Yes, please."

"You okay?"

"I'm fine."

He said nothing more and started driving me back to the party. I was really late now, but that could be a good thing. I was hoping everyone would already be knee deep in liquor. They would be far more willing to talk if alcohol had loosened them up a bit.

I walked into the party with my head held high. I needed to appear confident. I pasted on a smile and carefully adjusted the little box that was concealed under the belt of my dress. At least, I was hoping it was concealed.

I spotted Austin laughing at something a man was saying. It was his fake laugh. I didn't mind interrupting the conversation. I grabbed a glass of champagne and meandered over to where he was standing. I flashed a smile.

"If you'll excuse me," he said to the man he was talking to. He walked to me and made a big show of looking around. "You're missing someone."

"Am I?"

"Where's Cooper?"

This was an opportunity. "Cooper and I have decided to put our relationship on pause."

He smirked. "Pause?"

Yes."

"Let's get a drink."

I held up my glass. "I'm good." I wanted to control the amount of alcohol I drank. I could not afford to get even a little buzzed.

"So you're here all alone," he said with a smile that would normally melt my heart. Not anymore. My heart was hardened toward him.

"I am. You?"

"Yep."

I casually pulled him away from the crowd. "I wanted to apologize," I told him. My heart was pounding in my chest. I prayed the recording device was working.

"For?"

"Accusing you of stealing."

"I hadn't realized you accused me."

"The book. I knew it was plagiarized. I went to Wendy and Gary."

He raised an eyebrow. "Oh?"

"Yes. They assured me it was all good. They said you had done that for the first two books as well and the original writers had been compensated."

He was looking at me like he wasn't sure if he should admit to it or not. I prayed he would. I needed the proof. "I told you I didn't steal anything. I took a story, cleaned it up, elaborated on it, and made it my own."

Inside, my heart was jumping for joy. "I get it now. Gary said the authors had been compensated."

He shrugged. "I don't know the details. All I know is it isn't illegal."

"Did you find the books? I only realized the situation when I remembered reading the book you just recently gave me to edit. I showed you that book a while ago."

"Yeah. I read it and saw it had potential if I put my name on it." His cocky grin made me want to slap him.

"Well, I guess if everyone is happy. Although I got the impression one of the authors wasn't all that happy with the idea."

He scoffed. "She got paid. She tried to come back for more when the book made some real money, but that ship had sailed. She threatened lawsuits. She signed the paperwork giving me the book and a confidentiality agreement. No one has the money or clout to go up against me and the company."

I forced a smile. "Of course not. Easy money for you."

He winked and reached out to put his arm around my waist. "I like this dress." His hand settled on my hip. He frowned and looked at the belt. "What is that?" he asked. "You wired?" He flashed a grin.

"It's my phone," I told him.

He looked at the wide belt. "Weird place to hold your phone."

"It's an inside pocket since I don't have a purse. It's very forward thinking for ladies' fashion."

He nodded as if he could care less. "Why don't we go out to the garden?"

He wanted me alone. I was not going to let that happen. "I have barely made an appearance. I can't go stealing the hottest man in here."

That seemed to soothe things over, just like I knew it would. "We'll mingle for a bit and then I'm getting you somewhere dark and private."

I forced a laugh. "So did you come up with the idea to steal books or did they?"

"I didn't steal a book, Tatum."

"I'm sorry. I meant, was this something you saw to do?"

"Why?" he asked.

I was pressing too hard. "I was just curious. I wonder if it's something I could do."

He raised an eyebrow. "It's about the marketing. When I got busted with the book, they weren't mad."

"So you did try to pass it off as yours?"

"No. Yes. I mean, my agent was aware there could have been some borrowed bits. It didn't matter, though, because no one read the book. No one was ever going to know where it came from. Do you know how many books are out there right now?"

"Millions."

"Needle in a haystack." He grinned.

I couldn't believe I had been so fooled this whole time. "What did I always see you working on?"

He shrugged. "Just doing a few name and location changes. Little things to keep it from being picked up by some copyright thing."

"Copyright thing?"

"Yeah, like one of those websites that finds stuff like that."

"Austin, the book I read was almost identical. It only takes a few words in a row to trigger an alert."

He smiled and took a drink from his glass. "That's why the books are taken down. We wait a couple of months and then we publish with my face on the back cover."

"Wow," I said and shook my head.

"I know, right," he said with a laugh.

I couldn't stand to be in his presence another second. "I have to go."

"What? We're here alone. We both look good. Why not stay? Let's see where the night takes us."

I shook my head. "I have to get back."

"One more drink."

He wasn't going to just let me walk away, and I wasn't interested in causing a scene. I finished my champagne and handed him my empty glass. "I'm going to use the restroom. Can you get me something fruity?"

He grinned, thinking he'd won. "Hurry back."

I cut through the crowd, glancing back a few times. When I saw him caught up in conversation with someone, I veered to the right and rushed out the front door. I walked down the driveway and pulled my phone from the little pocket. I pulled up the Uber app and quickly ordered a ride without stopping my escape from the lavish house. I didn't want to risk Austin coming to look for me.

With my ride ordered, I quickly called Cooper. He didn't answer his phone. Again. Clearly I had a lot of work to do to try and salvage the relationship.

I decided to send him a text. *It's done.*

I hoped he would be waiting for me at my place when I got home.

Chapter Two

Cooper

I GLANCED DOWN AT MY phone when I came to a stop at a red light. I'd been driving around aimlessly since I left her place. I wasn't a fucking dog. I didn't appreciate being told to sit and stay. We had been friends before we were lovers. As her friend, I probably wouldn't have minded. As her boyfriend, it wasn't cool. I supposed I wasn't her boyfriend. We were more off than on, it seemed.

"It's done." I repeated the two-word text she'd sent. "What the hell does that mean?"

I didn't know if she was talking about us or if she was talking about him. It wasn't exactly clear. It confused the hell out of me. That wasn't anything new. She'd been confusing the hell out of me since I first met her. It was like this all the time. She always sent mixed messages. I blamed her for the pain I felt.

I couldn't deal with it anymore. I got off the freeway and found myself driving towards Damon's house. That was the normal thig for me to do when I was stressed. Burning gas all night wasn't going to solve this. It was time to shit or get off the pot. I couldn't keep going like this.

I got to Damon's house and knocked once. He opened the door, looked me up and down, and shook his head. "Shit, again?"

"Dude, I'm so fucked."

"Do you want a beer?"

"Like twenty."

"That bad."

"Yes. To both."

He walked to the fridge and grabbed two beers. I took the one he handed me and flopped down on the couch. "What happened?"

"She went to that fucking party."

"I thought you already knew she was going to go."

I took a long drink from the bottle. I was going to be crashing at his place. I could feel a good drunk coming on. "I didn't think she would do it. I went to her place. She was dressed to the nines in a short ass dress that damn near had her ass hanging out."

"Why didn't you go with her?"

"I wasn't exactly invited. And I cannot face that asshole without going to jail. I will fucking hit him. I'm so tired of that guy. He's been in my life for too long. I never liked him back then. Now he should not be a part of my life. I have nothing in common with the guy. I don't like him. The guy is a snake. Why do I have to keep dealing with him?"

"Because she is."

"Exactly!" I said and slapped my thigh. "He could be out of both of our lives. It isn't like they have children together. They didn't live together. There is nothing keeping him around. Except her."

"I think we have already established their long history kind of makes this difficult."

I rolled my eyes. "I don't see that. I wouldn't have a problem kicking my ex to the curb if necessary."

"Um, really? You haven't been able to put her behind you and you weren't even dating her."

"What is it?" I asked with frustration. "Does she know when she constantly chooses him over me it makes me think she doesn't want to be with me?"

"Have you told her?"

"I think I've made my feelings more than clear. I told her, directly to her face tonight, me or him. If she left, I was done. She asked me to wait for her like I'm a fucking dog to be ordered around."

"Why did she say she had to go?"

"It's still that revenge bullshit! Seriously, she's got to be the most vengeful woman I have ever met. I have never seen someone so hellbent on making someone suffer. It doesn't exactly give me the warm and fuzzies."

He laughed. "I would suggest you not screw her over."

"No shit."

"She's doing this for more than just one reason."

"How do you know?"

He shrugged. "Because you said so yourself."

"Yeah, but seriously, is she on a crusade? Why can't she just call the police or something? I don't understand why this is her personal responsibility. She says she loves me, but she is always with him. Doesn't that mean she is always thinking about him? If she loved me, wouldn't she want to spend more time with me?"

"Now you doubt her love?"

"I don't know what I think. She has me twisted up. I just wish there was a way to make Austin go away. I'm not talking like a hitman, but just go back to whatever hole he crawled out of."

"But you still love her."

"Yeah, well, I've loved her for years, and I've been just fine. It wasn't until I started messing around with her that shit got so messed up. I should have just left it alone."

He laughed and took another drink. "Do you mean to tell me you wish you never would have gotten to be with her these last few weeks?"

When he put it like that, hell no. I would never want to give up the nights we spent together. "No."

"Look, you've been going back and forth with this woman for weeks."

"I know. It isn't fair to you. I keep bitching at you. You've done nothing but try to tell me to pull my head out of my ass, and I can't seem to figure out how."

"I agree," he said with a laugh. "You need a roadmap."

"I don't know if that would help."

He got up and walked to the refrigerator before returning with two fresh beers. "I know I haven't exactly supported this relationship. It isn't because I don't like her. I do like her. I told you I didn't think it was a good idea to jump on this so soon after she broke up with Austin. I still don't think it was a great idea, but I did see you ridiculously happy for a few short moments. When things were good with you guys, you were in a good place."

I scoffed. "Both times?" I said with sarcasm.

"It has been limited. I say this because I think you need to hear it."

I knew what was coming. It was the same thing he always said. He would tell me to walk away and leave it be for a while. "Just say it."

"Figure it out, man. Seriously, figure out what you want. If you want her, go after her. Fight for her. If you don't want to fight, then walk away and call it a day. You keep asking me questions and telling me what you should be saying to her. Ask her if she wants this thing between you to work. I'm guessing she's going to say yes. Then you guys sit down and really hash out the details of this thing. You know her better than anyone else—put aside your feelings for her as a boyfriend. Think about her as the person you know her to be. Maybe then you'll understand her desire to go after this guy."

I gave him a look of confusion. "You're telling me to try and make this work with her? I thought you were against it."

"Not against it in general, but against how fast you jumped into things. I didn't want you to become the rebound. Obviously that's too late. I know you love her, and I believe she loves you. I just think you need to set a target and keep moving toward it. This other stuff is just noise. It's in the way. You need to clear the noise and focus on what could be. On what both of you want. If she needs time to get this revenge shit out of her head, then figure out if you can live with it. If you can't, you need to make a clean break. You can't go back and forth. It's going to turn you inside out. Again."

"Even if she constantly rejects me and ignores my wishes?"

"That's on you to figure out."

"How so?"

"Do you not believe she's doing this for the reasons she says she is?"

"For the little people?"

He nodded. "Yes. Do you think she's doing it because she wants him back?"

"No. I mean, I don't think so. You should have seen what she was wearing tonight. Who gets dressed up to catch their ex in a lie? Doesn't that seem a little excessive?"

"I don't know, you tell me. Better yet, ask her."

I supposed I might have been a little hasty to dole out an ultimatum. "I should have talked to her."

"Yes, you should have."

"It's just so damn annoying. She's always running back to him for this revenge nonsense. I can't help but wonder if she's making shit up just to be close to him."

"Again, you know her best."

I finished the second beer. "Damn."

"Maybe you should call her."

"She was at the party."

"So?"

I rolled my eyes. "I'm not going to call and sound like a sniveling idiot in front of Austin. He's about the last guy I want to know she dumped me to hang out with him. I've got some pride."

"Then leave her to him."

I knew what he was doing. He was trying to get me fired up. "The hell I will."

I grabbed my phone from my pocket and walked out the front door to get some privacy. I called her and waited for her to pick up. I wasn't sure what I was going to say, but I needed to say something. She didn't answer. I couldn't explain it, but that pissed me off more than her simply walking out the door.

I went back in the house and straight to the refrigerator and grabbed a fresh beer. "That good, huh?" Damon asked.

"She didn't answer."

He winced. "Damn."

"What do you think she's doing?"

"I have no idea, and I think guessing could be very dangerous. Give her the benefit of the doubt. If she's at a party, she might not have her phone on her."

I nodded, but my mind was spinning with the possibilities. I had no idea what she was doing. I wasn't going to assume she was doing anything with Austin, but her little plan to get him recorded saying things could have gotten dicey. I wasn't worried for her safety. It wasn't like Austin's scheme was worth hurting anyone over.

But I couldn't help but think about her and Austin. That dress. Austin's demands to leave his woman alone. He was making moves to get her back. Her whole revenge plan was based on him wanting her back. Now that he did, would she take him back? Would she remember the good times and want them back?

The very thought of her with him made me ill. Another beer would help dull the pain.

Chapter Three

Tatum

I GROANED, PUTTING a hand to my head. I'd drunk too much the night before. It was one glass of wine and then another, and before I knew it, I was drunk. I'd poured my heart out to Piper. I kept pouring and she kept pouring.

I rubbed a hand over my face to try and clear the fuzzy feeling I had. Her couch was actually pretty comfortable. Or maybe it was the amount of wine I drank that made it feel far more comfortable than it was. I would know when I tried to get up if there were any kinks.

It was early. Piper was most likely still asleep. We'd been up late last night. Me whining and crying about screwing up my life. I swallowed hard. I let myself feel the poor, jilted woman, even if I had done the jilting. I let myself feel like shit and I complained about how sad I was to have Cooper dump me. Again, my fault. He wouldn't have dumped me if I had just stayed put.

It had been a miserable night. I had replayed the moment I left him in my apartment over and over. He'd begged me with his eyes. He'd asked me to stay for him. I didn't. I walked out on the man that I knew really loved me. Austin never loved me. Not like Cooper. I walked out on the one man that could really make me happy. The man I knew would stick beside me through thick and thin—if I did the same for him.

"Good morning," Piper said with a yawn as she walked out of her bedroom.

"Hi."

"I'm going to make coffee. Really, really strong coffee."

"I'm sorry. I hope you don't have a deadline today."

"Nope. I'm good. The joy of working from home. I can massage my deadline a bit. I'll just work extra hard tomorrow."

I got up—slowly, very slowly, and started to fold the blanket she let me use. "Thanks for hanging with me last night. I got home and saw he wasn't there, and I just couldn't be there."

"It's okay. I'm glad I could be here for you. How are you feeling this morning?"

"Physically? Hung over and miserable. Emotionally, miserable."

She laughed. "Okay, coffee and toast is coming up with a side of Advil. That will cure the physical. The emotional part is on you."

"I know," I mumbled and walked to the bathroom. I splashed some cold water on my face and tried to clear the cobwebs from my brain.

When I returned to the kitchen, she had just put a couple pieces of toast on a plate. "Sit and eat. You've got about ten minutes."

I blinked. "What?"

"Are you going to work today?"

"Do I have to?" I groaned.

"Nope. Stay home and sulk."

"I'm not sulking."

She sipped her coffee and looked at me over the rim of her cup. "Today is a new day. You accomplished what you set out to do. I heard the recording. It's clear and very damning. You did a good thing. Cooper has to know that you are making a difference in the world. It might just be a teeny tiny ripple in the grand scheme of things, but you are helping out people that have been silenced by lawyers and money."

"If it even works."

"I am sure it will at least institute change. What they are doing is wrong. They won't go to jail for it, but they will have to change their practices, and that's what counts. You sacrificed to help others. That is something Cooper should admire you for, not be pissed at you."

"You know it isn't what I was doing that pissed him off," I said with a sigh. "It's how and who."

She shrugged. "But you got it done. If he doesn't want to believe what you were doing helped the world, that's on him. This is all on him."

"I hate this."

"I know."

"I felt like I was stuck between a rock and a hard place. I knew what was right and I knew what I really wanted, but I wouldn't have been able to keep working at my job if I had ignored this."

"I get it. I appreciate what you did. It will make a difference. It might not be newsworthy, and it might not be a huge game changer, but someone out there is going to appreciate not having their hard work stolen."

"Thanks. I hope it did someone some good because lord knows it pretty much ruined my life."

"Stop. Your life isn't ruined."

"Can I borrow something to wear?" I asked her. "I am going to be pushing it as it is."

"Of course."

"Thanks."

I took another bite of my toast and went in search of my phone. I tried to turn it on, and it was dead. I put it on her charger that was always plugged in. "Let's go raid my closet," Piper said.

I followed her into her bedroom. I wasn't interested in trying to look good. I was just trying to get through the day. She was a little thinner than I was, but we managed to find a maxi skirt and a pretty blouse.

I showered and used the makeup I had in my purse to put myself to-gether.

"You going to be okay?" Piper asked.

"I'm fine."

"Are you going to say anything to anyone at work?"

"No. Not yet."

"Be careful. I don't think I trust these people in the least. They are not good people, and they stand to lose a lot of money if you take this public."

"I know. I'm not saying anything yet. I've got the evidence, but I would like to get Wendy and Gary admitting to it as well."

"That could be risky."

"I know. I left the recorder at my apartment last night. I was going to wear it at work today. Maybe I should run home and grab it." I looked at the time and realized I was already going to be late. "Never mind," I murmured.

"Don't push it too hard. They might start to suspect something if you keep asking a lot of questions."

I nodded. "You're right."

"Do you need anything else?" she asked as she walked me to the door.

"No. I'm good. Thank you for last night. I'm sure you had much better things to do than listen to me whine about my boyfriend."

"I had nothing to do. Besides, you just gave me a little more fodder for my book."

My mouth dropped open. "No!"

She laughed. "Not like that, but the whole heartbreak thing is go-ing to help me get the emotions on paper."

"Gee, I'm so glad my disastrous love life is going to give you some-thing to write about."

"Me too." She winked.

When I walked into work, I was happy to see I wasn't the only one feeling a little green. I offered a few smiles as I made my way to my office. I almost got the door closed when Beth, a fellow editor, stopped me.

"Oh my goodness!" she squealed.

"Ow," I groaned and grabbed my head.

"Sorry." She grinned and thrust her phone in my face.

"What are you doing?" I said and took a step back. "Aren't you hung over?"

"I didn't go to the party last night. I was a good girl. You weren't."

"I was at my friend's house last night."

I sat down at my desk. She sat down with the same goofy grin. "I bet you were."

"What are you talking about?"

She slid her phone across the desk. "I didn't know you two were back together."

"Who? Who's back together?"

I picked up the phone and stared at the picture of me and Austin at the party the night before. I read the salacious headline that included his name, but not mine. I wasn't upset about it. I didn't care if my name was ever known to anyone.

"You guys look so happy," she said. "He is looking at you with such love."

I scoffed. "Yeah, right."

"Look at you smiling at him."

It was a fake smile. I had been playing a game. I didn't think anyone would be watching. "This is bad," I whispered.

"It's amazing! Wendy is thrilled with the idea of you two back together again. She is already working with marketing to come up with some ways to use this relationship to promote the new book."

I almost puked. "No."

"You guys look so good together. You truly look like you are in love."

A thought occurred. "Where is this on?" I asked.

She shrugged. "It's been on a couple of websites already and is picking up steam."

"Is Wendy pushing it?"

Beth rolled her eyes. "You know she is. This is free advertisement."

It was as if Wendy sensed we were talking about her. She opened the door to my office without bothering to knock. "There you are! I'm so happy for you."

This was a sticky situation. "Wendy—"

"I knew you two were meant to be. You guys are great together."

"I thought he was supposed to avoid being seen with anyone," I said. "Weren't you and his publicist in agreement that he should be single? Am I going to be harassed by his female fans? I'm afraid to read the comments on this."

"I wouldn't," Beth quickly advised.

Great. "We're not together," I said.

Both women looked at me like I was lying. "Tatum, we're not blind," Wendy argued.

"I needed something from him. I was pretending. I was going along with it."

"Did you get something from him?" Beth teased and waggled her eyebrows.

"Not that. I went home shortly after that picture was taken. He was flirty. That was it."

"That touch is very intimate," Wendy said. "Look at the way he is looking at you. That is a look of love."

"Lust. That is lust fueled by alcohol. He would have looked at anyone like that. In fact, I know he does. It's kind of why we broke up in the first place. I'm not interested in going back to that."

"Oh, come on now," Wendy said with a wave of her hand. "He made a mistake. He obviously sees what he lost, and he wants you back."

I scoffed. "Too bad."

"You don't think you could forgive him?" Wendy asked. "After all, men stray. It happens. What really counts is how well he begs for forgiveness."

"Not in my book."

"I think you look very happy with him," Beth said.

"I was trying to look happy."

"Looks like you played that part a little too well," Wendy said with a smirk on her face.

"I think that is going to end up biting me in the ass," I muttered.

"I have a call to make, but I like this, Tatum," Wendy said. "I like this a lot, and I think it could be a great way to drum up some free advertisement for the new book."

I forced a smile. It was about the last thing I wanted to help him with. To help any of them with. "I'll keep that in mind," I said.

"I have to get back to work, but I just wanted to say congratulations," Beth said. "And that dress! You looked amazing. His fans are going to be so jealous. Take that hate mail with a smile. That only means they are jealous of you because you are gorgeous."

"Yeah, just what I wanted."

She left my office, and I quickly googled Austin's name. "Oh shit."

This was not good. If Cooper saw this, we were absolutely over. He was never going to forgive me. The picture looked bad. I grimaced when I stared at another image that was taken within seconds of the first. We did look like we were sharing an intimate secret. If a picture could say a thousand words, I needed to have about ten thousand prepared to tell Cooper. I had no idea if he would even hear me out.

I might have had a chance to explain but not now. The picture was damning. It was going to be the final nail in the coffin that held my relationship with Cooper. The deck was stacked against me, and I didn't see a way out of it.

Chapter Four

Cooper

I LEFT WORK EARLY. I wasn't fit to be in public. I was pissed and hurt at the same time. After struggling to put together a shelf and throwing a screwdriver, I decided to call it a day. All because a couple of women were gossiping. I never listened to the many conversations that happened all around the gym while people worked out together. I tried not to, but when I heard Austin's name, my interest was piqued.

I listened to them pick apart his girlfriend. When they started complaining about the dress and the hair and the big tits, I didn't have to guess who they were talking about. I found myself wiping down the same machine over and over while I listened to them talk. Initially, I thought they were talking about her as his girlfriend in the past. Then when I heard them talk about last night, my biggest fear was realized. They kept talking about the picture and the party.

Then I did the one thing no one should ever do when trying to confirm a story—I searched the internet. I didn't have to look far. It popped right up. I got home and poured myself a stout drink. I settled in, and knowing I shouldn't do it, I did it anyway. I looked up the story once again.

I cringed when I saw the photo of the two of them. His hand was resting on her hip, his face inches from hers as she smiled up at him.

Did they kiss after the picture was taken? It certainly seemed like that was the next step.

My phone rang and pulled me away from the picture. It was her. "Yeah," I answered.

"Cooper, don't hang up."

"What do you want?"

"We need to talk."

"Not interested."

"Please, Cooper. Let me explain."

I couldn't get the image of them out of my head. I wanted her to tell me they were back together. I needed to hear it from her. "I'm at home."

"Can I come over?"

"Whatever."

The moment the call ended, the image of her and Austin came back on the screen. it made me cringe. It made me want to throw my phone at the wall. Instead, I took a straight shot of the rum before adding another shot to my glass.

When she arrived, I was feeling a bit more chill. The liquor had taken the edge off. I opened the door without saying a word and sat down in my recliner. My laptop was sitting on the small table next to the chair. I grabbed it and spun it around to face her. "You're famous," I told her.

She looked properly ashamed. "Let me explain."

"Oh, I don't think you have to explain. There are at least ten bloggers and journalists that have explained it all in great detail, right down to the brand of your dress."

"They don't know what they are talking about."

"I think they did a great job. Hell, they even got your drinks pinpointed."

"It wasn't what it looked like."

I put the laptop back on the table and stared at her. "It looked like you two were having a very good time."

"I was only playing along to get him to tell me what I needed. I had to play nice. I got it all on my recorder. Shortly after that picture was taken, I left. Nothing happened. The rumors are ridiculous. We didn't leave together or go outside together. None of that ever happened."

"Someone claims they saw you two kissing."

"They lie. I wasn't there. I left. I went home to see you. You were gone. Actually, I went back to the apartment before I ever went to the party, and you were already gone."

"I told you my feelings on the matter."

"I tried to call you. I texted you. You never responded."

I held up a finger. "Actually, I did. I called and you didn't answer."

"My phone was dead. I went to Piper's house last night."

I wanted to believe her, and I supposed I did in a way, but part of me was afraid to get involved. "You didn't go to the party but then you did go?"

"When I got back the first time and saw you weren't there, I figured I'd already pissed you off. I decided to go to the party and get what I needed. I had to make it worth it."

"Was it worth it?"

She blew out a breath. "Yes. No, but yes. I got what I needed."

"Congratulations."

I kept my voice calm. I was not going to let her see how badly I was hurting. I felt like my heart had been ripped out of my chest and stomped all over. I had to look away from her. I couldn't look at her. Seeing her hurt, knowing I could not have her the way I wanted her was beyond difficult.

"Cooper, I don't want Austin. I didn't go there to flirt with him or play games with him. I went there just to get the statement."

"You went there as part of another one of your revenge schemes."

"This isn't about revenge for me."

I shook my head. "I don't believe that for a second. You keep saying it, but I don't think it's true. You are invested in destroying him. He cheated on you. He treated you badly. That doesn't exactly make him a villain worthy of being taken down. You are hellbent on destroying him. You're either a little fucking psychotic or you want him back."

Her face was filled with shock. "I'm not psychotic."

"Then you want him back."

"No! I want you."

"If you truly wanted me, you wouldn't spend every waking moment thinking about him. How can you ever be with me if you are always thinking about him?"

"I'm not always thinking about him," she insisted. "It isn't like that. It's just this thing with the stealing of books. I can't let that go. I look at Piper and how hard she works. I look at so many other authors that submit stuff they've worked on for years. He's parading around like he's some talented author. He couldn't write two original sentences!"

"So?" I asked and shrugged my shoulders. "So fucking what if he is an untalented loser? How does that hurt you? How does his inability to write a book affect your life? Tell me, Tatum. I need to understand why you care so much about what he does."

"It isn't that I care what he does, but what he is doing to others."

"Turn him in and be done with it. Seriously, are you going to personally arrest him and then personally put the cuffs on him?"

"No."

"That's how you sound," I told her. "You sound like you are on this crusade all by yourself with you being the only one that can bring him to justice. You are acting like the superhero. Do you want a cape?"

"Cooper, don't be rude."

"I'm not being rude. I'm asking you a real question. I want to know why this is all on you to fix. You are being judge, jury, and executioner, and I have to believe that is because you want to be the one to punish him. You want to punish him because of what he did to you."

"No. I swear, it isn't like that."

"Tatum, we've been doing this dance for too long."

"What dance?" she breathed.

My heart was breaking as I looked at her. I saw the woman I had loved for as long as I could remember. "This. Me and you. Me always chasing you and you always rejecting me. You always chasing him. He dicks you over, you come running to me to console you. As your friend, I willingly did it even though I wanted to tell you to dump his ass. Whenever he hurt you, you came to me. When he was kind and kissing your ass, you ran right back to him, and I was left waiting for the next time he screwed you over."

"I didn't mean to make you feel used."

"You couldn't have used me if I wasn't willing. But you know how I feel. You've known but now you really know. I have let Austin be the ruler of my happiness for too damn long. I can't stand the guy and yet I have let him be the dictator of my life."

"What do you mean?"

"You. He gives you up and takes you back on a whim. You go. You let him dictate your happiness. That's on you. I won't do it anymore. Your life revolves around him. I let my life revolve around you, and it isn't working. You are trapped in his orbit, circling him like a planet circles the sun."

She didn't deny it, which hurt. "You are right. That was me in the past, but that's not me now. I've seen how much he has screwed me over. I'm sorry it took me so long to see it. I'm sorry I pulled you back and forth. That wasn't cool. I swear if I had known how much it hurt you, I wouldn't have done it. I feel awful for being so caught up in my own world. I was caught up, and I didn't see what I was doing to you."

"Don't pity me," I snapped. "I'm done."

"What?"

"I'm done letting him rule my life. He can rule yours if that is what you choose. You do you. I want no part of it."

"No," she said and jumped to her feet. She truly sounded anguished. "I don't want him to rule my life. I won't let him."

"Your actions say otherwise."

"You have to let me explain."

"You did. Unfortunately, I don't believe you. I saw the picture. Pictures, actually. In each picture, you are looking at him with such longing and love. That said it all. It's all I needed to see. I'm glad I've finally seen the light. It sucks it took so long, but I see it now."

She was shaking her head. "It was fake! It wasn't real. I was only trying to get him to talk."

"You keep saying that, but I saw the way you were looking at him. You forget, I've seen the way you look at me. I've seen the way you look at me when you want me to fuck you."

She flinched, and I immediately regretted my words. "Cooper, the way I look at you is genuine. You have to see the difference. Look at me. See me. I only want you."

"I saw you with him," I said in a hard voice. "I'm so glad I was able to help you get your man back. Your plan was a success."

"It wasn't a plan! I didn't want him back. I still don't want him back!"

I wanted to believe her. My heart was turning inside out watching her. I wanted nothing more than to pull her against me. I wanted to hold her. I wanted to kiss her and pretend that nothing had happened. It would be easy to take her back, but then, we would be right back in this place. We'd find ourselves back here, fighting about Austin. She worked with him, and it was clear he was going to go out of his way to make our lives miserable. He wasn't going to let her go, even if he didn't actually want her. He only wanted her because she'd been with me.

"I think you should go," I said. My voice was gravelly, reflecting the emotion I felt.

A tear rolled down her cheek. "Don't do this," she whispered.

"It's done."

"This isn't done. Don't say that."

"I'm not going to be your rebound. I'm tired of being used for one reason or another. I can't do it."

She was crying now, tears streaming down her cheeks. I wanted to cry with her. I felt the same pain, but I wouldn't show it. I couldn't. A single sign of weakness would make me vulnerable. She would spring, and I would be helpless to argue against her. She held a power over me that I couldn't explain.

"This isn't over," she said.

"It is."

"You were my friend first. Can't we be friends?"

"I don't think I can do that right now. I don't think I can be near you and not want to be with you. I need to end this."

"No! Hell, no. You don't. I'm here. I'm begging you. I'm putting myself in your hands."

I looked away. I couldn't look at her. She wiped her tears and walked out the door without a word. I squeezed my eyes closed and blew out a breath. My heart hurt. Every fiber in my being was telling me to go after her. I wished I didn't love her. My life would be so much easier if I could just let her go and not think twice about it. If I could only turn off the feelings I had for her. I hated that she was upset, but I was certain she'd get over it. She'd be back in Austin's arms by the end of the week. Just the thought of that pulled at my heart in a way I could barely stand.

Instead of dealing with the feelings, I walked into the kitchen and poured another drink. It probably wasn't the healthiest, but it was better than the alternative. It was better than chasing her down and professing my love.

Chapter Five

Tatum

I FELT SHATTERED. I wasn't sure if I felt worse because I was fresh on the heels of being shattered by Austin or if this was more intense because I felt so strongly for Cooper. This was different. I had hope before. I didn't feel any kind of hope now. Before, I had Cooper to help me through. Now, I was certain I'd lost him for good. I wouldn't even have him to call friend.

I groaned and rolled to my side, pulling my blankets up to my eyes. I was once again curled up in my bed and feeling miserable. Cooper and Piper weren't going to come through the door and cheer me up. I was on my own. I was on my own with no one to tell me it was going to be okay.

I glanced at the clock. It was just after two in the morning. I had yet to sleep. I'd been in bed since I left Cooper's house, but I couldn't fall asleep. I kept replaying everything he said. He acted so cold. He acted like he was well and truly finished with me, but I was certain I saw something in his eyes. That is when he deigned to look at me.

That's what hurt the most. He couldn't even look at me. I saw the flashes of pain when he talked about me choosing Austin. I knew I'd hurt him. I hated that I'd hurt him. That was never my intention. "Does anyone ever intend to hurt the ones they love?" I asked myself.

Of course not. It just happened. Selfish choices hurt the ones we loved. Choices that didn't put the loved one first hurt them. It was like walking a minefield. I threw off my blanket and gave up trying to sleep. My mind was running a million miles per hour, and sleep was not going to happen.

I went into the kitchen to make some chamomile tea. I didn't think it would work, but I was willing to try just about anything. I needed sleep. I needed the oblivion that came with sleep. I sat down at the table with my phone in hand. I read through the message chain between Cooper and me. I smiled at some of the sweeter messages. A few slightly dirty messages were mixed in as well. It was all more proof of what I'd lost. I tossed it all away because I had this need to do what was right.

I exited the messaging app and found myself online. I checked Instagram and almost immediately saw my own face. That was just a little disturbing. "Don't do it," I murmured.

I did it. I started to scroll through the comments. I winced as I read them. People were cruel. They were keyboard warriors with no regard for other people's feelings. I followed a link to a blog. It was a fan page dedicated to Austin.

"Ouch!" I read a scathing post about me cheating on Austin and him taking me back. The writer had a lot of information about our relationship, except the part about Austin cheating on me. The blogger failed to write about the girl Austin had been seen with the last few weeks.

I read through the comments on the post about how I was ruining Austin's career. Commenters were not interested in talking about Austin's books or the new one that had been the talk of the previous posts. Nope. They wanted to know if my tits were real.

"Asshole!" I read one comment from a so-called doctor. There were side by side pictures of my boobs from a picture that had been taken from my own Instagram page and put alongside the picture taken from the party.

I couldn't believe what I was reading. They claimed my tits were fake and I had butt implants. "I'm not a Kardashian!"

I had put on a few pounds and filled out a bit and I was automatically accused of getting cosmetic surgery. The fans hated me. It was like they thought Austin was actually their boyfriend, and they were pissed that I'd stolen him.

I shut off my phone. That had been stupid. I shouldn't have looked. Now I felt just a little more miserable. I crawled back into bed and huddled under my blankets with the hopes the world would just fade away. I never knew emotional pain could physically hurt.

I must have dozed off at some point. When I woke up, my alarm was blaring. I reached over and slapped at the box. I couldn't go to work. I did not want to be seen, and I did not want to see anyone. I decided to use one of the many sick days I'd been banking.

"Wendy," I said when she answered. I wasn't faking the harshness in my voice. It was all very real. My emotional trauma had left me feeling like I'd been run over by a truck.

"Tatum? Is that you?"

"I'm calling in sick," I told her.

"You sound like hell."

"I feel like it. If I can, I'll try and work from home, but I make no promises."

She let out a long sigh. "It's fine. Do what you can, and I'll see you tomorrow."

"Yeah, tomorrow," I said and ended the call.

She was partially to blame for this. Her deception was all part of the scheme to screw authors over. Austin wasn't in this alone. I didn't want to be anywhere near her, especially after she tried to push me and Austin back together. She had seen me with Cooper and had been all for that relationship until she wasn't. Until she realized Austin and I could drum up free publicity for his stolen book.

"Thank you," I muttered and put my phone down.

I wanted to sleep. I'd probably gotten two hours, and it wasn't nearly enough. I needed to block out the world. When I closed my eyes, I saw Cooper's face. I saw him smiling at me. I could taste him on my lips. I could practically feel him inside me. I couldn't handle the thought of never having him again.

The smile I was so used to seeing on his face morphed into the last look he'd given me. The combination of hurt and anger as he ordered me out of the house. It was an image that was forever burned into my soul. I couldn't get it out of my head. If I couldn't have him back, I hoped I could at least get him to forgive me and be my friend again. I knew that was unlikely, but I couldn't stand the thought of him hating me.

I tossed and turned before throwing off the blanket once again. I couldn't sleep. I showered before pulling on a pair of lounge pants and a loose shirt. I made myself another cup of tea and sat on the couch. I stared out the window, not really seeing anything. I drifted off, thinking about everything and nothing.

As much as I didn't want to, I thought about the shit I read on the internet about me. About Austin. About his talent. They hated me now. When the truth about him and my role in the takedown of him and everyone involved was revealed, shit would really hit the fan. I would probably have to move. I would need to fall off the grid. If his fans attacked over a silly picture of the two of us together, what would they do when they found out I had secretly recorded him? The picture they fawned over was nothing more than part of the setup.

"Shit. I might have to move out of state."

I looked around the apartment I called home and started making a mental list of the things I would sell to make the move easier. There was nothing to keep me in LA. If I couldn't have Cooper, I didn't want to stay. I didn't want to run into him. I didn't dare risk seeing him move on with another woman. It would kill me.

I couldn't say how long I sat on the couch staring and thinking and staring some more when there was a knock on the door. "Cooper," I breathed and jumped up.

I knew he would come to his senses! I wiped my face before rushing to the door. I jerked it open and felt the sigh escape me. It was such a letdown. "Austin," I said. "What are you doing here?"

"Damn, you do look sick."

"What?"

He didn't wait for me to invite him in. I closed the door and turned to look at him. "I went by the office. Wendy said you were out sick."

"Oh."

"Did you see all the press?" he asked with a smile.

"You know that was not what it was."

"But it can be," he said.

I shook my head. "No. Why are you really here?"

"You look like you could use some company."

"I'm fine."

"I'll make you some soup," he offered.

I smirked. "You mean you'll open the can?"

"I can dump the contents of the can in a pot," he said with a laugh. "Come on, sit down and let me take care of you."

"No, Austin. I just want to be alone. I have a migraine. It's why I called in sick."

"I won't yell. I'll just hang out."

"No thanks," I muttered.

He sighed. "Fine. I need my USC sweatshirt back. I have a book signing there in a few weeks. With all the press, I want to be spotted wearing the shirt before the signing."

I looked at him. "Why?"

"So they like me."

I rolled my eyes. "I don't know if I have it."

"You do. You wore it home just before—"

I raised an eyebrow. "Just before you dumped me?"

"Yes."

"It's probably in my closet."

"I'll get it," he offered.

"No! I'll get it."

I walked into my bedroom and opened the closet. It only took a second to find it. I had washed and folded it and stuck it on the shelf with several other sweatshirts. I snatched it and carried it back to the living room. He was staring at his phone, probably reading more about the picture.

"Here," I said and pushed it at him.

He turned his phone for me to see. "It just got picked up by the mainstream news. This is great!"

I had to ask. "Why? Why is it great now, but when we were together, you didn't want anyone to know we were together? What changed?"

He shrugged and put his phone back in his pocket. "I don't know. I guess they were wrong."

"Who was wrong?"

"My publicist. Wendy. My agent. Everyone. They were certain my fans wanted me single. They thought if I was taken, it would put a damper on the interest in me. If I'm single, they had a chance."

It was so ridiculous. "And now?"

"Well, I have to be honest, not all of the fans are cool with the idea of me and you being together."

"Because they think you can do better," I muttered. "I read the comments."

He actually smiled. "That's just the jealousy talking. They'll come around."

"They don't need to come around. We aren't together."

He stepped forward, putting a hand on my chin before kissing my forehead. "Yet."

I tried not to flinch at the contact but the thought of him touching me made my skin crawl. He was not the man I wanted touching me. "Goodbye, Austin."

"I hope you feel better soon. I'll call you later."

He had the sweatshirt in his hand as he walked out the door. Hopefully none of his crazy fans were stalking him. The last thing I needed was them figuring out where I lived. I did not want that kind of drama. I locked the door and went back to the couch to sulk.

I needed to get all of Austin's things together. That would eliminate these little visits to collect this or that. He could have just bought a sweatshirt. I wasn't dumb enough to believe his excuse. He'd come over because he wanted to talk about the press. He loved when he was talked about. He loved to see his name in the press.

Every time I saw him now, I tried to understand what I'd seen in him before. What made me fall in love with him? What made me think I needed him? I thought my world was over when he broke up with me. I felt so stupid and foolish now. The whole time Cooper had been right there, and I'd never really noticed him. I didn't notice him until I *noticed* him. Now I could never go back.

Chapter Six

Cooper

I STARED AT DAMON'S phone. I shouldn't have been surprised. I wasn't actually shocked to discover they were spending time together. I knew they were. I had seen the proof with my own eyes. It was foolish to think there was a chance.

"Nice," I said and pushed the phone out of my face.

"What the hell is that about?" Damon asked.

"It's fine. We ended things. I knew she was back with him."

"You ended things?" he repeated. "Like for good or is this another one of those off times?"

"It's over."

He looked at his phone and shook his head. "Man, I've been there."

"Been where?"

He grinned. "That's the morning after look. It's a step above the walk of shame. He's in a hurry to get home or back to work or whatever. He probably went over last night."

He may as well have kicked me in the gut. "Why do you say that?"

"Because he went over when it was chilly. He is leaving this morning when it's warm."

"Are they sitting outside her building?" I snapped. "Is he really that important?"

"She's going to be internet famous at this rate," he laughed. "Maybe that's what they both wanted."

"You think she did this on purpose?"

"Did what?"

"The whole breakup thing?" I asked. It was hard to accept, but I was also thinking the same thing.

"Yeah. They broke up and then she used you to get revenge, but what if it wasn't about getting revenge and more about getting him back?"

"I know. I've thought about that same thing."

"She wanted to show him she could get a guy like you. He got jealous, which was expected. When he went after you, it was exactly what she wanted."

I didn't need to hear him echo it. "It's done now. I don't care."

He scoffed. "Bullshit. You are all twisted up about this."

"I'll get over it. I told her last night it was done. She tried to tell me the picture wasn't what it looked like."

"What was it?"

"She said it was nothing more than a brief moment. It wasn't what it looked like. It was innocent. She was innocent. She said she loved me."

"Do you believe her?"

I wanted to say yes, but deep down I didn't think she did. "No," I answered honestly. "I believe she loves me the way she has loved me all these years. She sees me as a friend and will only ever love me as a friend."

"But the sex? Don't try to say you didn't have sex."

"I'm not talking to you about that."

He scoffed. "I wasn't asking for the dirty details, but if you wanted to give them I wouldn't be sad. I was only asking if you thought she used you for that as well."

That stung more than it should have. I knew I had been used and used plenty of women for the simple act of getting off. I wanted to believe it was more than that, but there was a lot of doubt surrounding everything I thought I knew about her.

"I don't know."

He nodded, telling me he could read between the lines. "And now you have further proof she is back with him."

"I suppose I do. I won't listen to any more excuses. I was dumb enough to hear her out last night. I won't do it again. I asked her to leave."

"And what did she have to say about that?"

The sadness in her eyes still haunted me. "It doesn't matter. It's over."

"I guess I was right all along."

I glared at him. "Don't talk shit about her. I might not be with her, and I don't know that we are friends, but you don't get to disrespect her."

He held up his hands in surrender. "I won't, but if you need a shoulder to lean on, I'm here."

"Thanks. I've got a client coming in."

I excused myself and walked away. I could have gone all day without seeing that picture of Austin leaving her place. He was carrying a sweatshirt. His dark sunglasses did little to disguise his appearance. I didn't think he was trying to hide who he was. He was smiling and looked a little too put together to have just rolled out of bed. I was certain it was set up. He wanted a photographer to catch him leaving her house. It didn't mean I didn't think there was nothing going on, but it looked like he was trying too hard.

"Asshole."

"Excuse me?"

I spun around to see Jill standing with her hands on her slim hips. She was wearing her usual workout attire of spandex from top to bottom. She had the figure for it and looked amazing. "Sorry, I was speaking out loud."

"Are you okay?" she asked and reached out to put a hand on my shoulder. I was used to her very hands-on approach.

"I'm good."

"You sure? You don't look like you are having the best day."

"It certainly hasn't been one of the better days of my life."

"I'm sorry to hear that. Do you want to talk about it?"

I shook off the sadness. "Nope. I'm good. Let's get you moving. It's been a while since I got to make you sweat and beg for mercy."

She giggled in her usually flirty way. "I've been waiting for this day. I'm glad to be back, but I haven't been slacking. Gary had that gym put in at the house. I've been staying up on my cardio."

"Good. Then we can work you a little harder."

"No, no," she said with a laugh. "I want to be able to walk out of here."

"We'll see," I said and walked with her to the treadmills.

I pushed her through a grueling workout. I was right alongside her, sweating and breathing hard. When the workout was over and we were doing our cool down, she started making small talk again. "How is your girlfriend?" she asked.

"I don't have a girlfriend."

"You know who I'm talking about," she laughed. "I saw her briefly at the party, but I never got the chance to talk to her. I was hoping you would have been there."

"No. I didn't go."

"I think I've hit a sore spot."

"Tatum and I are not together. Not anymore."

"That was fast."

"We're better off as friends."

"That's too bad," she pouted. "I liked her."

"Me too," I muttered.

"I can't be too sad. It means there is still a chance for me."

I laughed. "I don't think your husband would appreciate that."

"My husband is a busy man. A woman needs attention."

"You should tell him that."

"Oh, he knows. His work keeps him busy. I can't really complain because that work keeps me living very well. It also pays for these little sessions."

"Then I guess we better let him work."

"And I need to keep this ass high and tight or he might trade me in for one of the little gold diggers that are always sniffing around."

"We won't let that happen."

"Are you sure you are okay?" she asked again without any joking.

"Thank you for asking, but I am fine. It's just been a shitty day."

"I'm sorry, sweetie. You're a good man, and any woman would be lucky to have you."

"Thanks."

After she left, I took a few minutes for myself. The pictures of her with him and him leaving her apartment kept flitting through my head. I couldn't get the images out of my mind. How many more pictures was I going to have to see? How many more times would I have to see her with him? When would it stop hurting so much?

I wanted to feel something other than sadness. I wanted to tap into the anger and drown out the hurt in my heart with real pain. I headed back out to the gym floor and hopped on a treadmill. I cranked it up, running at full speed. Sweat dripped down my back and pooled at my waistband. I kept running, as if I could somehow run away from the problem.

I ran until my legs felt like they were going to fall off. I wasn't done with the punishing workout. I hopped off the treadmill and managed to walk on legs that felt very weak to the punching bag hanging from the ceiling. It was my favorite exercise. I pulled on gloves and took a few deep breaths before I unleashed holy hell on the unsuspecting bag.

I jabbed and hit, grunting and groaning. I could feel the tension rolling out of me. Anger bubbled inside me, rising to a fervor that left me almost blinded. I didn't need to see. I felt the bag and knew where to hit. I relied on my instincts. Pounding the bag until I felt a hand on my shoulder.

"Cooper," I heard Damon say.

I stopped hitting and turned to look at him. He looked worried. "Shit, man. I've been trying to get your attention for several minutes. What the hell are you doing?"

I wiped sweat from my brow with the back of my forearm. "I was just getting a workout in."

"You looked like you were trying to kill that bag."

I was breathing hard. So hard I felt a little dizzy. I leaned forward and put my hands on my knees. "It was just getting good."

"Go home."

I popped my head up. "What?"

"You are not okay. Go home. Take a minute to get your head together. Get drunk. Cry. Do whatever you need to do."

"I'm fine."

"No, you aren't."

"Stop."

He stepped closer, his eyes darting over my shoulder. "You just beat the shit out of this bag after you did a run on the treadmill that would have made Usain proud. You're freaking out the clients. You obviously didn't notice, but they're watching. You look like a madman. You're bad for business."

I turned around and noticed the looks. They were trying hard not to stare, but they were watching me. I couldn't ignore it. "Sorry."

"It's fine. I'll handle the last client on your books. Go home and take it easy. With the workout you just put yourself through, I doubt you'll be standing much longer."

The adrenaline was fading. I was feeling the after-effects of my workout. "Fine. Whatever. I'm fine, but I'll go." I took off my gloves and tossed them on the bench.

"I'll see you tomorrow."

"Yeah," I mumbled. "We'll see."

"Do you want me to come by after I'm done here?"

"No."

"Why don't we go out for a drink? It will help get your mind off her. A pretty brunette with a wild personality is exactly what you need."

I scoffed. "It is the last thing I need. I don't want to go out."

"Don't sit alone and think about her."

"I have no intention of doing that. I've got shit to do. I still need to fix the bathroom sink. She is going to be the last thing on my mind."

"If you say so" He smirked.

I walked into the locker room and caught a glimpse of myself in the mirror. I was drenched in sweat. My hair was a little wild, and my hands were red despite the gloves protecting them from the bag. I stared at my reflection for several long seconds. I could not let her do this to me. I was not going to turn into a nutcase because she was playing games.

I stripped out of my wet clothes and took a quick shower. The run was really taking a toll. I went out the back way without saying a word to anyone. I was pissed I'd let my emotions get away from me. I had not meant to let anyone see my frustration and pain. It made me feel weak. I didn't want him to look at me with pity.

Chapter Seven

Tatum

"WHERE WOULD IT BE?" Piper asked.

I groaned and tugged at my hair. "I don't know. It was on the table. I left it there after I got home from the party. I listened to the recording. I went to your house, and I swear it was there yesterday."

She nodded. "Okay. You need to sit down. Let's go over the night you got home from the party. Have you used or moved the recorder since then?"

I shook my head. "No. I had no reason to. I went to work. Then to talk to him and then home. Yesterday I pretty much lay on the couch all day. I went to work this morning and when I came home to get it for the meeting, it was gone."

She stood in my living room and looked around. "We are going to be late."

"I know," I groaned again.

"I can call them and ask if we can reschedule."

"The lawyer for the two authors is not going to be happy," I said.

"There is nothing more to do."

"I am going to look like such an idiot. I reached out to the author of the book with the promise of proof. Now I have nothing to show for it. They are going to think I'm screwing with them."

"They aren't going to think that," she assured me. "They know you are trying to help them."

I threw up my hands. "I'm of no help. Just because I tell them what he told me; it doesn't make it true. It will never stand up in court."

"Isn't the recording on your phone?"

"I didn't download it. I didn't want to risk anyone getting my phone and finding it on there. It's stored in the memory of the recorder." I slapped my hands over my face. "I really screwed this up."

"Relax. Let's look again. Maybe you were absentminded and put it a drawer."

She started pulling open one drawer after another. I got down on my hands and knees and scanned the floor. There was nothing but a few dust bunnies. I got back to my feet and scanned the room with fresh eyes. My jacket was draped over the back of the couch. I searched the pockets. I knew there was very little chance it would be in there, but I had to look. I had been a little distracted lately.

"Oh no!" I gasped.

Piper spun around. "What's wrong?"

"Austin!"

"What about him?"

"He was here yesterday. I know that recorder was sitting on the table. I went in the room to get his sweatshirt. He was alone for a minute. He had to have snatched it."

Her eyes widened. "No way. You think?"

"It's the only explanation! Oh shit, if he has it—" I couldn't finish the sentence. The possible endings were all bad.

"Shit! What do you think he's going to do?"

"I have no idea. I have to get it back."

"I don't think you can just call and ask for it back."

"What am I going to do?" I moaned and flopped on the couch with my arm thrown across my face.

"You're going to have to play nice."

I shook my head. "I can't do that. I am not going to give him a chance to get another picture of me with him. I know he set that shit up yesterday. Cooper is never going to believe me if we keep getting photographed together. I can't fix things with Cooper if I don't prove to him there is nothing going on."

"Hon, that ship has long sailed."

"What?"

"I don't mean to be rude, but after the picture yesterday, I think it's pretty unlikely he is going to take you back."

I sat up and looked at her. "Uh, that's rude."

"It's the truth."

"You could lie to me. Give me some hope."

"I don't do hope. I deal in facts, and it is very unlikely he is ever going to want you back."

"Holy shit, Piper. That's rough."

"I'm not trying to hurt you, but I think you need to be honest with yourself. You need to move on. You are going to be stuck in this seesaw nonsense for a long time if you don't accept things for what they are. It's better if you stop hoping for something that won't happen."

"Gee, remind me not to call you when I'm standing on the edge of a cliff."

"You know I love you. I love Cooper. You two gave it a go, and it didn't work. I don't want you both to suffer."

She was speaking the truth, but it still stung. I couldn't accept there was no chance for us. I tried. I tried to tell myself it was well and truly over, but it was one of those things that just wouldn't die. My heart was full of hope. It was because I knew Cooper so well. I knew he was a good man. I knew he had loved me for years. I couldn't imagine that love had just gone away.

"This is going to suck," I muttered.

"You're doing it for a good cause."

"If you say so."

I grabbed my phone and called Austin. I felt a lump of nausea in my throat. "I've been waiting for your call," he answered.

I was glad it was a phone call because if he would have said it to me in person, he would have seen me curl my lip. "I was at work."

"Want to get dinner tonight?"

I had to close my eyes and swallow the bile in my throat. "Sure. I'd like that."

"I'll pick you up."

"Oh, I'll have to meet you there," I blurted it out before I could think of a good excuse.

"Tatum, that isn't a date."

"I'm sorry, I have to meet Piper to go over her outline." Piper smiled and waved a hand to encourage me on. "But I'd be happy to meet you at say seven?"

"Wear something sexy," he said and ended the call.

I dropped my phone on the couch. "Gross. I can't believe I have to have dinner with him. I just know he is going to have photographers there. Cooper—"

Piper held up her hand. "It doesn't matter if Cooper sees the pictures. Now, get your purse. We need to get to that meeting. We'll tell them we have the recording. We don't even know if they are going to move forward with it. The lawyer might not be able to find a way around the NDA. If things go well, we'll get them the recording."

I nodded. "Then I have to get back here and get ready for my date. I cannot believe I have to go on a date with him. So gross."

"Just play nice."

"Am I supposed to come right out and ask him if he took it?"

"You could casually bring it up and see what he says."

"I'm not a very good spy."

"You could just leave it be," she said, knowing damn well I wasn't going to do that.

"If he listens to that recording, he's going to know I recorded him on purpose."

"Just tell him you were wearing it for me. I wanted you to do some research."

I smirked. "Yeah, that's plausible."

We left my place to meet with the attorney and author before I had to rush back home to get ready for my date with Austin. My skin crawled just thinking about sitting at a table with him. I dressed in a simple black cocktail dress. It was one I had worn before with him. I didn't care if he wasn't impressed with it. I didn't want to impress him.

I walked into the restaurant and gave my name. Austin was already at the table sipping a glass of wine. I put on my game face and sat down. "You look nice," he said. There was a pause like he searched for a word.

"Thank you. I wish I would have had time to buy something new."

"Me too."

"How are you?" I asked. I forced a smile and told myself to pretend I liked the guy.

"I'm good. Did you see they caught me coming out of your place?" He said it like it was a bad thing. I knew he set it up. I knew it made him happy.

"I did. They must have followed you."

"Everyone with a cell phone is a paparazzo. Someone must have snapped it with a cell phone. I didn't even notice."

"Do you think someone is taking pictures of us right now?"

He grinned. "Probably. Thankfully, you look beautiful and will photograph well."

I had no idea how I was going to eat a bite. I was sick to my stomach at the very thought of spending a minute with him. He ordered me a glass of wine despite me telling him I didn't want one. I sipped on it throughout the meal. He talked nonstop about his accomplishments, including the boat he was going to buy with his coming bonus after his book was published.

"Why don't we go back to my place and I'll show you the brochure," he offered.

I had to remind myself I was playing a role. I could do this. "I'd like that."

He quickly paid the check and left a generous tip. As we were walking out with his arm around my back, I was certain I saw someone take a picture of us with their phone. Our instant fame was heightened with every one of those pictures. At least until there was a real Hollywood couple to chase around. Five years ago, I would have been thrilled to be the girlfriend of a famous author. I would have loved to be seen out and about with him.

"Why don't we ride together?" he said.

"I drove here."

"Leave your car."

"I have to work in the morning. I'll be right behind you."

He left it alone. I followed him back to his place. When we got there, I was absolutely certain someone photographed us walking into his place. All I could think about was Cooper seeing the pictures. Cooper seeing me going into Austin's place. It was going to piss him off and hurt him. Like Piper said, it didn't matter. It was done and over with us.

"Can I pour you a glass of wine?" Austin asked. "Or are you giving up the hard stuff?" he teased.

"How about something a little stronger?" I said in a sultry voice.

"It isn't like you have to drive home. You might just want to stay the night."

I forced a smile. "Maybe."

"I'm going to use the powder room," I said and walked out of the huge living space. While he was making drinks, I was going to search his room. I did a quick search and didn't find it. I quickly went into the bathroom, flushed the toilet and ran the water before going back to the kitchen.

He handed me my drink. "Thank you." I walked to the windows that overlooked the city from his penthouse. "I've missed this view," I said aloud. I actually hadn't meant for that to come out. I did miss the view. I didn't miss the apartment or the man in the apartment, but I missed the view.

"It's a million-dollar view. I'm going to change. Do you want me to grab you something more comfortable to wear?"

I knew what he was saying. "Not yet," I said. It was a way for me to give him hope without actually committing to anything.

"Put on some music. You know where the controls are."

"I will," I replied. It was the perfect excuse to search his place.

I casually walked to the table next to the couch with the tablet that controlled the lights, TV, AC, and everything else. I pulled up the playlist I knew he loved. The room flooded with music. I turned it up a few notches to cover the sound of me ransacking his place. When he walked out of the room, I furiously searched the area. I glanced over at the entryway table and rushed to it. I pulled open the drawer and found the recorder. Relief flooded me. I snatched it and stuffed it in my purse before he returned.

"How's the drink?" he asked.

He had put on a pair of sweats and was now shirtless. The man was attractive, but I just wasn't attracted to him. "You look comfortable."

"I am. You sure you don't want to change out of that dress? At least take off your heels."

I wanted nothing more than to run out of the penthouse, but if I did, he would suspect I'd found the recorder. It's placement in the drawer told me he knew I would want it back. I had no idea if he listened to the recording, but I suspected he had. Or he was planning on it.

I kicked off my heels and moved around the room. I didn't dare sit down. If I did, he would make a move. I needed to stay on my feet, literally and figuratively. "Do you have a press tour scheduled?" I asked.

"Yep. It's a doozy this time."

"You like that," I reminded him.

"I do. I love meeting the fans."

I had to bite my tongue. They weren't his fans. They were the fans of the sweet, young girl I'd met earlier tonight. Tabitha was real author. The people he'd met were her fans. Not his.

"Sit down," he said as he took a seat on the couch. He grabbed the tablet and turned down the lights.

I sat in the chair. "I should really get going," I told him. "I have a really early morning."

"Stay," he whispered.

"I can't. Not tonight."

"Tatum, I want you."

Words I would have killed to hear weeks ago. Now, those words made me want to run out screaming. "I'll see you later. Thank you for dinner."

I managed to get out of the penthouse with only a small amount of protesting from him. I got in my car and let out the breath I'd been holding. I checked my purse to make sure the recorder was still in there. It was. I'd gotten it back. Mission accomplished.

Chapter Eight

Cooper

IT WAS ALMOST TEN O'CLOCK, and I knew I should go to bed. Sitting and stewing wasn't going to do anyone any good. At least if I was asleep I didn't have to stress. I could be blissfully unaware of life happening around me. I wasn't in a good place, and I didn't want to see all the other people in the world enjoying their lives and loving relationships. I couldn't even stand to watch TV. All of it was a reminder of what I didn't have. I didn't think I would ever have it. Try as I might, I couldn't bring myself to completely hate her. I couldn't bring myself to truly accept it was done and over between us.

When I heard a knock on the door, I went on high alert. It was too late for regular company. It had to be Damon. He was probably coming to see if I'd destroyed my house in a fit of rage. When I peeked out the window to verify it was him before I opened the door, I was just a little surprised to see Tatum standing on my stoop.

My first reaction was to ignore her. I didn't want to hear it. She'd done enough damage. But I was a glutton for punishment. I found myself opening the door and staring at her. She looked up at me, her eyes turbulent.

"Can I come in?"

I made no move to invite her in. "Why?"

"I'd like to talk."

"I think you've said all I care to hear."

"You haven't heard me at all. Please let me explain."

I looked her up and down. "Date night?"

"Cooper, please. I swear this will be the last time I try and talk to you. You can kick me out when I'm done, but I need to say this."

"Oh goodness, I would hate for you to not get what you want."

"Please," she said, and it felt like her hand was on my heart and twisting.

I looked behind her. "Where's your boyfriend? Do you have paparazzi following you?"

"Are you going to let me explain or not?"

"You've explained several times. It's always the same story. I'm not sure how things are going to change."

She reached into her purse and pulled out a small black box. "This changes everything."

"What's that?"

"Proof."

"Of?"

"Proof of why I was doing what I was doing," she answered.

I knew Tatum well enough to know she wasn't just going to go away. She was going to stand on my doorstep until she said what she needed to say. I opened the door and stepped to the side. "Let's get this over with."

She stood in the living room. I didn't invite her to sit down, and I didn't sit. I wanted this over and done with as quickly as possible. I wasn't interested in hearing another story about revenge. I was hoping she would get the hint, say what she had to say and go on her merry way. It was cruel for her to keep coming back and screwing with me.

"Your lover may not appreciate you being here," I said. I couldn't resist taking a jab.

"He isn't my lover."

"The pictures say otherwise. You can't deny the proof."

"It isn't real," she insisted.

"Looked real enough to me."

I sighed and shook my head. "Whatever. Real or not real, I'm tired of seeing the proof and then hearing your excuses. It doesn't matter. You are free to date who you want."

"Sit down."

"Excuse me?"

"You heard me. Sit down and listen to me. I'm done being pushed around."

I smirked. "I don't think I'm pushing you around."

She walked to the couch and sat down. I blew out a breath and followed her. "I really can't keep doing this," I told her.

"I know. I expect nothing from you. I want you to hear me out. I know you don't believe me, but I got the recorder. I have the proof that backs up my story. You can't believe everything you read on the internet. A picture taken out of context is not the whole story."

"I think those single pictures say a lot about what was happening."

"No, they don't. I told you that night the picture of us that was taken at the party was not what it seemed. His hand was touching the recorder. In that moment, he was asking me what it was." She held it up. "It was this. I'd like you to listen."

I wasn't interested, but she was going to do it anyway. The room was filled with her and Austin talking. I could hear the background noise of the party and then, like a skilled interrogator, she managed to get him to spill his guts. "Good job," I told her when she shut it off. "You got what you wanted. That doesn't explain why he stayed the night."

She rolled her eyes. "He didn't stay the night. He came over to get his sweatshirt. Yes, I know he used the sweatshirt as an excuse. He was at my place for less than five minutes. I told him to leave. I wasn't feeling well. He left. The picture was obviously staged. He is just feeding the fanfare."

"But you know he is doing that. Why do you keep giving him the opportunity to use you as a publicity stunt?"

She held up the recorder. "Because I am using him."

"To take him down."

"Not take him down but lift up the authors he's screwed over. I have to believe other authors on the payroll are doing the same thing. I need the publishing company to be held responsible for this horrible practice."

"I think you're finding excuses to talk to him."

"Really? The lawyer I met with earlier today is pretty certain me getting close to him and getting the proof is going to make a huge difference."

"You met with a lawyer?"

"I did and two of the authors that have had their work stolen," she said with a smile. "But before I get into that, I need to tell you something else."

"Great."

"I had dinner with him tonight," she rushed the words out. "But it isn't what you think. He stole the recorder when he was at my house. I had to get it back. I agreed to go to dinner and then back to his place. I found it. Once I got it, I came straight here."

It shouldn't have pissed me off, but it did. It made my heart pound. "I see."

She slid off the couch and onto her knees in front of me. She grabbed my hands. "Cooper, I promise you, nothing happened. I don't want him. I don't want to even talk to him, but I had to get this proof. I know how it looked. I hated that it hurt you or made you think I wanted him. I am so over him. I'm not trying to get revenge on him. I'm trying to get justice for people that don't have the means to fight back. I would love for you to meet the lawyer and the writers. One of them is a single mom just trying to find a way to support her kids. Do you think it's fair that Austin is getting rich off her work? She didn't understand there were options. I want to help her."

I looked into her eyes. I believed her. I had to look past the pictures. I had to strip away my feelings and jealousy and remember who I was dealing with. I knew her, and this was exactly what she would do. If we were still in the friend zone, I would have supported her on this mission. I was letting my own feelings cloud my judgment.

"You did that," I said with a soft smile. "You're really helping a complete stranger."

"I'm trying to. Please, Cooper, believe me when I say there is nothing between me and Austin. He's playing games with me. At least, that's what he thinks he is doing. I don't want him. I only want you. I don't see him as a man I thought I loved. I see him as just any other guy on the street. You are the only one I want to be with."

I believed her. "I'm an ass," I said and cupped her cheek. "I'm sorry. I got caught up in the jealousy. I love you so much. The thought of losing you to him made me a little crazy. I never thought I was a jealous person, but I guess I am."

She smiled, her beautiful eyes filled with the love I knew she had for me but couldn't see through my green-tinted jealousy glasses. "I promise, you never have any reason to be jealous. There is no man out there that I want. Only you."

I bent down and kissed her. I was an idiot for letting myself get caught up in the drama. I only had to look at her. See her. Know her. Trust her. I slid my hands to her waist and slowly drew her up. We stood in my living room and kissed like there was a chance we might never get to kiss again. My hands slid around to her back and pulled the zipper of her dress down. I pushed it off her shoulders and let it pool to the floor.

"I want you," she breathed. "I need you."

"You have me. You always have me."

My clothes were stripped away until we were both standing in our underwear in my living room. I took her hand and led her to my bedroom. My hands slid over her silky skin, touching and tasting her. I laid her on my bed and took a moment to stare down at the woman who had the power to make or break me. It was a lot of power to give someone, but I wasn't afraid of it. Not anymore.

"Make love to me," she whispered and raised her hand to touch me.

I dropped over her, covering her body with my own and kissing her. The full body contact nearly had me coming without ever entering her. She writhed under me, moaning as her legs wrapped around me. "I want you more than anything in this world."

"You have me. All of me. I'm yours."

I rose up on my arms and stared down at her. Her blond hair fanned out around her, giving her an angelic appearance. Her lips were red and bruised with the force of my kisses. Her eyes were heavy-lidded as she stared up at me. I slowly slipped inside her. I reveled in the feel of her body opening for mine, the sweet, wet heat that enveloped me as I pushed inside her inch by inch.

"I burn for you," I groaned.

"More," she breathed and reached up to grab my shoulders. "Don't stop. I need you balls deep."

How could I possibly resist such a request? "Hold on," I hissed.

I thrust once. Her body slid under me. I thrust again and listened to her gasps of pleasure. Her legs locked around me as I thrust over and over. I claimed her body and soul with my own. I rode her hard and fast. What started as sweet lovemaking turned into something far more carnal. I had to have her. I had to show her how much I wanted her.

"Oh! Yes!" she cried out. Her nails scored down my back. I couldn't stop. I felt like my body was in control and I was just along for the best ride of my life.

"Fuck me," I growled when I felt the first bursts of liquid fire coat my dick.

"Don't stop!"

I couldn't have stopped if I wanted to. I was out of control. My body relentlessly pounded against hers. The sound of skin slapping against skin surrounded me. It was our own sweet music. She screamed out my name and arched up. Her juices coated me as her pussy clamped down on my dick buried deep inside her. I was lost in the moment. I gave her my all, exploding deep inside her womb.

I collapsed beside her, my body still twitching as I dragged her into my arms. "Wow," I managed to say.

"No kidding. Wow."

"I'm sorry for the way I treated you," I told her. "I was an asshole. I didn't trust you. That's on me. You were only doing what you knew was right. I'm sorry I didn't give you the benefit of the doubt. I love you. I know you know that, but I don't know if I can properly express just how much I love you. When I thought you were going back to him, it almost killed me."

"I'm sorry you felt like that. I promise you, I have no plans for revenge. I did at first, and that was wrong. I should have listened to you. I can't give this up now. I have to see it through. I want you to be able to trust me."

"I do trust you. I'll probably still get jealous, but I promise I will keep it to myself."

She rolled over on top of me, her chin touching mine. "I kind of liked the jealous thing. It was hot."

I grinned. "Then you are in for a real treat, because I've got all kinds of jealousy stored up."

Her soft laughter floated around the room. She kissed me, and I knew I was forever lost to her. There would never be another woman for me.

Chapter Nine

Tatum

THIS WAS WHAT LIFE was all about. I was happy. Like the kind of happy that made me feel like I was glowing from the inside out. It wasn't just about the sex. Although the sex last night had been amazing. It wasn't that it was wild or crazy, it was just the two of us sharing our hearts and souls. It was far more impactful than hot monkey sex. I was still planning on one of those nights in the near future, but for now, I was very content to ride the high of our rather sleepless night.

I yawned, covering my mouth before reaching for my phone. I pushed the contact for Piper and waited for her to pick up with my gaze focused on my office door. "Hey," I said when she finally picked up. "Did you hear anything?"

"No. I've left two messages, and no one has called me back."

"Shit," I hissed. "They probably think I'm yanking their chain about the recording."

"Or the lawyer is in court. Don't panic yet. This is on them. You have the evidence they need to pursue this thing. You shouldn't have to chase them down."

"But after our first meeting, they probably think I'm a fruitcake."

"Then it's their loss," she said. "Give them a couple of days. She is the one that is paying for that lawyer. Maybe she can't afford him.

Maybe the lawyer doesn't think he can get around the NDA. You did your part. Let's let the chips fall where they may."

"Because that sounds like me," I said dryly.

"Change of subject, what are you doing tonight?"

"I'm not sure. I'm going to guess it will involve Cooper."

She groaned. "You two are the epitome of a yo-yo relationship. Up and down and all around."

"This time it's legit. He's not going anywhere, and neither am I. Austin cannot do a damn thing to break us up. We are in it for the long run."

"Good. Let's go out to dinner. All of us."

"I'll ask Cooper, but I'm up for it."

"Good, I'll be bringing a date."

I laughed. "I knew there was an ulterior motive. I didn't know you were seeing anyone."

"I'm not. Not yet anyway. This will be our first date. If it goes well, there could be a second date."

"You want to bring a first date on a double date?" I questioned. "Isn't that a little weird?"

"Nope. I need a buffer. I've been striking out on the man front lately."

"Ah, so you are using us."

"Yes, but it will be fun too. You get to hang out with me."

"I'm thrilled. Who is this guy?"

She sighed. "Just someone I met at a coffee shop. I was working and he kicked up some small talk. He asked if I wanted to go out to dinner. I told him I would think about it."

"He asked you out, not all of us."

"Any man I date needs to know you and get along with you. I figure it's better to find out right from the get-go. I don't have time to waste. My biological clock is pounding. If he's not a keeper, it's better to catch and release instead of playing with him only to find out later you hate him."

I had to laugh. "I don't think I would hate anyone you were into."

"Trust me, it happens. I don't want you to go through what I went through with you and Austin. For the record, I hated the guy. I always thought he was a snake, but I played the dutiful best friend role. I don't want you to do that. If you think this guy is a snake, tell me. I will trust your judgment."

"I'm both flattered and offended," I laughed. "What's his name?"

"Vance. He's a software tech or something like that. Thirty, sexy as sin, and funny."

"Well hell, he sounds like your man. Why are you wasting time hanging out with us?"

"Did you hear the part about him being sexy as sin?"

"I did."

"If it's just the two of us, I'm going to jump him bones. Then I'm going to get into a fast and furious sexual relationship, and I won't even know if I like him. I need you to buffer as well as run interference."

"I feel so used."

"You'll be fine. Let's say seven at Bigis."

"I'll check with Cooper."

She made a sputter sound. "He's your man now. This is part of the rules. You get to tell him you're going out. Period. End of story."

I laughed. "I'll keep that in mind. I'll text you if he has a session."

"Tell him to cancel it."

"Yeah, I'll do that."

Fortunately for Piper, Cooper was available. I spent the rest of the day keeping my head down and doing my best to avoid Wendy. I wasn't sure I could hide my guilt. I shouldn't have been the one feeling guilty. If the lawyer did decide to move forward to sue Wendy and the rest of the heads at the company, things were likely to get very ugly for me. Assuming they knew I was the one that blew the whistle.

I wasn't going to worry about that. Not right now. I was going to focus on the positives in my life. Cooper. He was my man, and that was pretty fucking awesome. I was glad Piper had requested a late dinner. I managed to run by a little boutique shop and pick up a new dress. It wasn't overly sexy, but I knew Cooper was going to love it. The scoop neck showed off just enough cleavage to tease him. It was his favorite color and enhanced the bluish green color of my eyes.

"Do we have to go?" he asked in a husky voice when I answered the door. He put his hands on my hips and backed me into my apartment before devouring my neck with his mouth.

I groaned. "She'll kill me if we don't show up."

"I'll protect you."

"Tempting. So tempting, but after. You can bring me home, and I might just let you sneak a goodnight kiss."

"I'm going to sneak a lot more than that."

I slapped away his roaming hands. "We need to go or we are going to be late."

When we got to the restaurant, Piper was already there with Vance. She shot me a look that said she wasn't happy with my tardiness. I gave a slight shoulder shrug. "Hi, Vance," I said and shook Tall, Dark and Sexy's hand.

"It's nice to meet you. You look very familiar to me."

"Because she's an internet star this week," Cooper said dryly. "I'm Cooper. That's my girlfriend Tatum."

I loved how he called me his girlfriend. I loved how he staked his claim like it wasn't a big deal. It was a huge deal. My heart was leaping for joy.

"An internet star?" Vance said. "That sounds interesting. I know I haven't watched any porn, so something else."

Piper giggled nervously. I could tell she really liked the guy. I was happy for her. "Definitely not porn."

"I'll figure it out." He was staring at me, which was just a little awkward.

"I think I'd like a glass of wine," I said.

Cooper nodded and raised his hand. Our waiter came right over. It was when I had my glass in hand that Vance snapped his fingers. "That's it!" He pulled out his phone and nodded. Then he looked at Cooper with confusion.

"It's not what it looks like," Piper said.

I looked at Cooper, praying he wouldn't get mad. "She's with me," Cooper said. "Don't believe everything you read on the internet."

Vance laughed. "I see."

"It's a really long story," I added.

"If Piper agrees to go out with me again, maybe she can tell me the story."

His eyes flashed mischief as he looked at Piper. He was really into her. Piper was crazy not to want to date this guy. I understood why she wanted us to tag along. The guy was serious eye candy.

"We'll just have to see if you behave yourself tonight," Piper teased.

"I will be on my best behavior."

"So what do you do Vance?" Cooper asked before taking a drink from his draft beer.

"I design software."

Cooper nodded. "You don't look like someone who spends their days behind a computer screen."

Vance grinned. "I do, but I don't. I've made a good living doing what I do, which allows me the flexibility to work from my boat or the beach or at certain coffee shops when I'm in pursuit of hot authors."

The guy was into her. The chemistry was sizzling. I looked at Cooper. He was picking up on it as well. It was an aphrodisiac. I couldn't wait to get him back to my place.

"You are one smooth talker," Piper said with a laugh.

"Is it working?" he shot back.

"We'll see. I'm still deciding if I like you. I don't care for the really sexy guys."

We all laughed. The verbal sparring between them was nothing more than foreplay, and we all knew it. I had no doubt in my mind she was going to be taking him to bed very soon.

"What do you do?" Vance asked Cooper.

"I'm a personal trainer. I'm co-owner of a small gym downtown."

Vance nodded. "That explains the biceps."

Cooper laughed. "I have to be a walking advertisement."

"And he is an excellent advertisement," I said with a smile. I loved that I could say that now. I could say it and claim him as mine. Those biceps were mine. That sexy smile and chiseled jaw were all mine. "We should order," I said. I was suddenly in a rush to get dinner over with.

Cooper flashed a smile. He knew exactly what I was thinking. We ordered, and our meals were delivered rather quickly. The small talk was easy. I liked Vance. I had a feeling there was going to be a happy relationship in Piper's future.

"Thank you for the invitation," I said to Piper. "It was fun."

"Shit," Cooper muttered.

I raised an eyebrow. "Something wrong?"

He didn't get a chance to explain.

"You bitch," Austin seethed.

I looked up, shocked as hell to see him. "Excuse me?"

"Walk away," Cooper hissed.

"What are you up to?" Austin snapped. "You're out with him? On a double date? I got a phone call letting me know my girlfriend is cheating on me!"

"I'm not your girlfriend."

"The press thinks we are together! You're cheating on me!"

"Austin, keep your voice down. You're making a scene."

"You already did that. The photos are already on the internet. I look like a total idiot."

"You're doing a great job of that all on your own."

Cooper got to his feet. At first, I thought he was going to fight him. That was the last thing I wanted. "Cooper," I warned.

He pulled out a hundred dollar bill and left it on the table. I watched as he circled around Vance, who was still sitting and watching the show. Cooper very casually brushed past Austin and reached out to grab my hand. "We were just leaving."

I stood up, afraid Austin was going to make it physical. Vance rose to his feet and threw down his own cash. Austin was sandwiched between the two men. They both towered over him. Piper got up and hooked her arm through mine and gently pulled me away from Cooper. "Let's go," she said.

I noticed the phones and knew we were being recorded. This was my moment to hold my head high and walk away from Austin once and for all. I wanted the world to see me leaving him in my wake.

"Leave her alone," I heard Cooper say.

A moment later, his arm was around my shoulders and pulling me against him as we walked out of the restaurant. I didn't know about the rest of them, but my heart was racing. I was both elated and a little terrified. I didn't trust Austin. There was a damn good chance he would come after us. Cooper ushered me into his truck and started for my place.

Only then could I breathe. Austin was behind me in all ways.

Chapter Ten

Cooper

"YOU'VE GOT THAT SMILE again," Damon said as he walked into the office we all shared.

"I'm happy. That's the smile."

"I'm glad everything has worked out for you two. I'm afraid to ask, but do you think it will last?"

"Fuck you."

He burst into laughter. "I'm kidding. Really, though, is this something you think is going to last?"

I nodded without hesitation. "I do. Absolutely. I just have to trust her and trust my gut."

"I envy you and don't envy you, if that makes sense. I don't think I want someone to have my heart."

"It's not so bad."

"Eh, you've been a wreck the last few weeks with a few bright spots. I don't think I like the wreck part."

"You have to have the downs in order to enjoy the ups."

He smirked. "Yeah, I enjoy the game and getting laid without worrying about who is supposed to call who the next day. Youth is fleeting. I want to use this face and this body while I have it."

I laughed and shook my head. "You're going to wear that body out at the rate you are going."

He winked. "I'll keep that in mind."

He walked away and I got back to work. I pulled up the spreadsheet for my next client and made some adjustments in preparation for the coming session. When I heard my phone ring I hoped it would be Tatum. She often called throughout the day. I liked our little chats about nothing.

I glanced down and saw Austin's name. He never called me. The only reason I had his number in my phone was because of the few times Tatum would be with me and he couldn't get her on her phone. usually because she was ignoring me. I thought about not answering it, but if I could get him to talk to me and leave her alone, I would do it.

"Hello?" I answered. I would be civil. Until he stopped being civil.

"Cooper."

"Yes, Austin. You called me. What do you want?"

"I know what she did," he hissed.

"What the hell are you talking about?"

"Don't play dumb with me. I know what she's doing, and she isn't going to get away with it. She thinks she's so smart. She's about to find out what happens when she messes with the wrong person."

"Fuck you, Austin."

He hung up before I could say anything else. "Shit," I hissed. He knew. I didn't know what he had planned, but I needed to warn Tatum.

I called her right away. When she answered, I could tell she was crying. "Tatum, are you okay?"

She sniffled. "Yes. No. I'll be okay."

"Austin just called me."

"I'm sorry," she sniffled. "I just got fired."

"What?"

"Austin listened to the recording and found out what I was going to do somehow. He called my boss and told her everything. I've been fired, and they are threatening to sue me for all kinds of reasons."

"Where are you?"

"I'm packing up my stuff."

"I'll come and pick you up."

"No, it's fine. Piper is already here. She's going to take me home."

"I'll cancel my sessions and be over."

"Cooper, you don't have to do that. Piper will be with me. Just finish your day, and I'll be there when you are done."

"Are you sure?" I asked her. "I don't mind canceling my plans."

"It's okay. Wait, why did Austin call you?"

"I'm not sure exactly. I think he just wanted to piss me off."

"What did he say?"

"He just said he knew what you did. He hung up without saying much of anything else. Just had to get the last word in. Fucking prick. I should go to his place and kick his ass."

"Don't do anything that might end up with you getting sued. Just come to my place when you are done."

"I will. I'm sorry, baby. This sucks. I love you."

"I love you. See you tonight."

I ended the call and stared at the phone. I would have loved to call Austin back. I wanted to tell him I thought he was a royal prick and a thief. He deserved to be thrown in jail. I hoped like hell Tatum and her little recording managed to bust his ass. I hoped he had to pay back every penny he'd essentially stolen from the real author.

I headed for the gym floor and tried to focus on my work. My poor clients got the workouts of their lives. I pushed them hard and joined in with them. I couldn't stop thinking about how sad she had sounded. I hated that she was suffering. I wanted nothing more than to go to her. Damon was taking my last client of the day. She didn't need to know I was cutting out early.

"Thanks again," I said to Damon on my way out. "I'll take your early client."

"Yeah, you will."

I stopped by the store and picked up a bottle of wine and a bouquet of pretty spring flowers. I remembered her penchant for ice cream and grabbed a variety of flavors before heading to her place.

"Hi," I said when she opened the door. "I brought supplies." She looked rough. Her nose was red and her eyes puffy, but she didn't seem to be in too bad of shape.

She smiled and opened the door wider. "You are too sweet."

"Shift change," Piper said and got up from the couch.

"Don't let me run you off."

"No, no," she said. "I've got a hot date with chapter thirty-three." She hugged Tatum. "It's going to be okay. The good guys always win."

"I hope so," Tatum muttered. "I'm not feeling very hopeful at the moment."

Piper offered me a smile. "Take care of her."

"I will."

After she left, I pulled Tatum into my arms and held her close. "Thank you for coming," she said.

"You know I'm here for you. Like she said, the good guys win. You'll get through this."

"Let's bust into this wine," she said and stepped away.

I opened the bottle and poured two glasses while she put the ice cream in the freezer. "We ordered pizza," she said. "Want some?"

"Yes, please."

We sat down on the couch with our pizza and wine. "How are you really doing?" I asked her.

"Honestly?"

"Yes."

"I'm a little freaked out."

"About him?"

"No. I don't care about him."

"What are you freaked out about?"

"I'm jobless. I have not been a good little girl and saved up for a rainy day. I have enough for a short time, but I need to find a job. Unfortunately, Gary and Wendy have threatened to have me blackballed. I don't know if I will ever get a job in publishing again. I worked my ass off to get that editor job and now it's gone. It isn't fair."

"You didn't want to work for them anyway," I told her. "They are unscrupulous and con artists. A reputable publishing company would be glad to have you."

"Maybe."

"How did Austin know what you were planning?"

"I don't know. He heard the recording. I'm sure he figured it out. He knows it's wrong."

"I'm sorry."

"It isn't your fault. You did tell me not to do it. I should have let it go."

"No," I told her and squeezed her hand. "Definitely not. I was wrong to tell you to drop it. You did the right thing. It's going to work out."

She snorted. "I might be homeless by the time it does."

I sipped my wine and thought about what she was going through. I could do little to get her job back for her. I couldn't force Austin to take it all back, but I could help ease her stress. "You're worried about money?"

"Well, of course I am. I am not independently wealthy."

"Move in with me."

She choked on the wine. "What?"

"I'm not going anywhere. I'd like to think you are not going anywhere. It isn't like we don't know each other. We spend every night at my place or yours. Move in with me. My house is plenty big for the both of us. It will take a little pressure off you. You won't have to worry about paying rent. Take some time to deal with this nonsense and then you can get back on your feet."

"That is very nice, and I appreciate the offer, but I can't."

"Why not?"

"Cooper, we've been back together for a handful of days. It's kind of soon to jump right into living together."

"We've known each other for a long time. I know your habits and you know mine. You know my quirks, and I promise I will put the seat down."

She laughed and leaned up to kiss my cheek. "You really are a good man."

"But?"

"But I can't do that. I'm not ready for that."

"Why not?"

"Because we just started dating. I don't want to scare you away."

"You couldn't chase me away with a big stick."

She laughed again. "I'll think about it. I'm not saying I never want to get there, but I don't want to rush things. I like who we are. I like our relationship. I like staying over at your place and you staying over at mine. I like my freedom."

"I get it. I do. I won't pressure you into anything, but just know it's an option. I don't want you to stress over how you are going to pay rent. I want to help."

"You being here is a huge help. You brought me ice cream. And flowers. That was exactly what I needed."

I kissed the top of her head. "I'm here for you. Whatever you need, I'm here. I'll help you in whatever way I can."

"Thank you."

"Are you still going to go through with it?" I asked her. "The threat of a lawsuit is pretty significant. No one would blame you if you wanted to walk away. You did your part. The ball is in their court."

She shook her head. "No way. I'm not backing down. No way am I going to let him get away with this. It was one thing to screw with complete strangers, but now he's come after me. I'm going to go after him."

"You're sure?"

She pulled away and turned to look at me. "Cooper, I swear to you, this isn't revenge. I mean, it is, but it isn't. I didn't start this thing for revenge, but now that he has cost me my job and reputation I want to kick his ass any way I can."

"I don't blame you in the least. He needs his ass kicked. What's the next step?"

"Unfortunately, I can't do anything for at least two weeks. The lawyer that was going to handle the case backed out. He didn't think it was worth going up against them. She found another lawyer willing to take the case, but the earliest appointment we can get is in two weeks."

"All right," I said with a nod. "And then it's over?"

"It's over. It will all be over and behind us. I won't be looking back. I will not pine for Austin or even think about him again. It's over."

"I believe you. We'll ride out the storm together. If Austin calls you, I want to know. We'll get a restraining order if we need to."

"I'll be fine. He thinks he got the last word. I cannot wait to see him go down in flames. That fancy penthouse is going to be gone. He told me he was going to buy a boat with the sales from this next book. Not going to happen."

I had to laugh at that. "Good. You know there has never been any love lost between the two of us."

"I do know, and I wish I would have listened to your advice a little earlier on."

"We all make choices that lead us to where we are right now."

"I wouldn't want to be anywhere else. I feel very lucky to have you."

I kissed her again, pulling her close to me. "We are going to make this work. Austin cannot take away the happiness we have together."

"No, he cannot. He can take my job, but he can't take my happiness."

I took her wine glass from her hand and put it on the table with mine. I got to my feet and pulled her up. "I think I'd like to make you really happy."

She smiled and leaned into me. "That sounds like a very good plan."

Chapter Eleven

Tatum

I WOKE UP IN HIS ARMS. It was the best place to be. It certainly made me think more about moving in with him. I would like to wake up with him every morning. But not yet. That was a huge leap. I didn't want to move in with him because I had no other options. I didn't want him to offer his home to me out of obligation. He was a nice guy. He was noble and would give a total stranger the shirt off his back.

I ran my hand over his chest. He moaned softly. "Don't tell me it's morning."

"It is."

"I think I like waking up with you," he said and smoothed his hand down my back.

"I know I like it."

"What are your plans for the day?"

I sighed and rolled to my back. "I don't know. I can't believe I don't have a job. I don't think I've quite gotten my head around the idea."

"You could take it easy. Curl up on the couch and enjoy a little TV. Watch all the Pitch Perfect movies. Read a book."

I scoffed. "I don't think I can read a book right now. It's going to remind me I am no longer a part of that world. I don't get to bring stories to life. I'm just a reader."

"Just a reader? That's not a bad thing."

"I'm never reading another book from that company," I said vehemently. "I will not give them a page read or a penny in sales."

"Good for you."

"I should probably look for a job, but I have a feeling it will be a waste of time."

"I can't imagine they can really blackball you. Your work speaks for itself."

I threw my arm over my face. "I think they can. I think I could apply for a job and I'll never get a call back. I just cost myself my career."

"I don't think that is true. Have a little faith in yourself."

"What time do you have to be at work?"

He rolled to his side, propping his head on his hand. "Do you want to come with me?"

"To the gym?"

"Yeah, why not? You can work out. Watch other people work out. Whatever you want."

I thought about it for several seconds. Normally, I would laugh in his face, but these weren't normal times. "Sure."

He grinned. "Really?"

"Considering my schedule is pretty damn clear today, I may as well. I promise not to get in your way. I'll just sit back and ogle all the hot guys that go through there."

"The hell you will," he growled and grabbed my breasts. "There will be no ogling."

I giggled and rolled away. "Just a little ogling."

"I'm going to make coffee," he said and got out of bed. I paused at the bathroom door to admire how hot he was. He bent over to grab his underwear off the floor. He caught me looking and smiled. "See something you like?"

"I do. I like a lot."

"You're right, we can't live together."

"Why not?"

"Because I'm pretty sure I would never get out of bed. I'm going to walk away now, but I warn you, if you are not dressed when I come back in here, all bets are off."

"Remember, I don't have a job. I have nothing to lose by staying in bed all day."

"Mean," he muttered and walked out.

I took a quick shower. As much as I would have loved to crawl back into bed with him, I wasn't going to make him late for work. One of us needed a job. When I got out of the shower, he was leaning against my kitchen counter with a cup of coffee in his hand.

"All yours," I told him.

"A minute longer and I was going to get in that shower with you."

"I wouldn't have kicked you out," I teased.

"Don't tempt me."

He got ready in under thirty minutes. I was kind of excited to watch him in action. When we got to the gym, he gave me a quick tour before he had to get into a training session.

"How are you?" Damon asked me.

I looked up from the desk Cooper shared with several other trainers. "I'm good."

"I was sorry to hear about the trouble yesterday."

"Cooper told you?"

He nodded. "He did. He didn't get into a lot of details."

"I suppose I should have known it was coming. I knew there was no way they would let me keep my job after I tried to take them down."

"Why don't we get in some time on the treadmill?" he offered.

"Don't you have clients?"

He grinned. "Cooper has all the clients. I'm just the pretty face."

I laughed and followed him into the gym. Cooper was focused on the young man he was working with. Damon got me set up on the treadmill doing a comfortable walk. I watched Cooper. I watched him encourage the guy and push him to lift the weight on the bar.

"Ready to go a little faster?" Damon asked.

"I don't think I can."

"Sure, you can," he said and reached over to turn up the speed.

I managed to keep up but just barely. I was never going to be a gym rat. I was never going to be one of those people who claimed to love working out, but this wasn't so bad. It felt good to sweat. It was oddly cathartic to feel my heart pounding in my chest.

"This is amazing!" I exclaimed.

"Get it, girl!" Cooper shouted from across the gym.

I grinned but didn't dare wave. I would fall on my face if I tried. Just seeing him smile at me gave me the energy I needed to push harder. I pumped my arms and felt free. I wished I could fly, but since the likelihood of me sprouting wings anytime soon was slim to none, this was the next best thing.

Damon gave me a little more training before we went back to the office. "Do you do all the paperwork?" I asked him.

"No, not really. It's a divide and conquer thing."

I looked at the desk that was stacked with papers. "Is there anything I can help with? I temped as an assistant before I got the editing job."

He shrugged. "Do you know how to do invoicing?"

"If you show me the program, I can figure it out."

"It's pretty self-explanatory. I would love the help."

"I'm all yours!"

He gave me a quick rundown and then left me to work on clearing the piles on the desk. It felt good to do something useful. I wasn't much of a paper pusher, but I could definitely get used to working twenty feet away from Cooper. As much as I'd loved my old job, it was unlikely I would actually get another job in a publishing company. I'd betrayed the trust of my company. No one would want to hire me. They would be worried I would do the same thing to them.

I had to accept the fact my career as an editor was over. I could do the odd job here and there, but it wasn't likely I would ever get to work in the publishing world again. I firmly believed in the old adage that when one door closed, another opened. I couldn't dwell on the loss of the career I'd worked so hard to get. It was over. Now it was time to pick up the pieces and move on.

It was a couple of hours later when Cooper came in. His hair was wet, telling me he'd showered. "How many times a day do you shower?" I asked him.

He shrugged. "Depends on the day. Usually two. Sometimes three. Especially grueling days, it could be four."

"Damn."

"I don't mind being a little sweaty, but my job often requires me to be up close and personal with clients. I can't be stinky when I'm direct-ly in their personal space."

"Good to know."

"Are you ready to go?"

"You're done already?"

"Yep. I'm ready to go. Do you want to go to my place or yours?"

I thought about it for a second. "Yours."

"Should we go by your place and get you a change of clothes?"

"Please."

As he drove through the city, I reflected on my life. Last night I'd shut him down about moving in together. Today, I was able to see a lit-tle more clearly. I'd rejected the offer to move in with him based on the old me. The old me was yesterday. Today was the new me. The me that had examined the situation and realized he was right. It was inevitable that we would live together. Denying him was essentially saying I didn't trust the relationship to stay strong.

"Did you enjoy yourself today?" he asked when we came to a stop at a red light.

"I did actually. Who knew sweaty bodies could be so cathartic?"

He laughed and reached across the center console and grabbed my hand. "You know you are welcome to hang out at the gym anytime. Damon said you unburied us from our backlog of paperwork. Thank you for that."

"Sure. It was easy."

"You know, you can edit. You can file. You can do invoicing. Why don't you start your own business?"

"My own business?"

"Yes. Why not? You can select your clients and decide how much you work. You might not make as much money as you did at your old job, but you'll get there."

"You are so good to me," I said.

"I will always do my best to be good to you."

We stopped at my place, and I packed a bag. I packed for a few days just in case I decided to stay over. It wasn't like I had anything waiting for me at my house. I thought about my future as he drove to his place. I had choices to make.

"You're quiet," he said.

"Sorry. I was just thinking about things."

"Do you regret it?"

"I'd be lying if I said I didn't regret it a little. I regret losing my job and my place in the publishing world. I don't regret calling them out for their wrongdoing. It needed to be done. I might be poor, but at least I'll have my integrity. I like being able to sleep at night. I'm not sure I could sleep soundly knowing what they were doing there."

"I think you are doing the right thing. I really do. I know I said otherwise, but I do think you had to do it for your own sake."

"No good deed goes unpunished."

"Nope. Have you thought anymore about what I mentioned last night?"

I looked over and smiled at him. "I have."

"I hope I didn't add any more stress to your already complicated life."

"You didn't. After I got over the initial shock of it, I realized you weren't off base."

"I'm not?" he asked with surprise.

"No. Waking up with you this morning was like waking up in my new life. I liked being in your arms. I realized I wanted that every morning."

"You do?"

"I do. It makes sense. I don't want you to think I'm going to be a mooch. I will get a job and I will pull my own weight."

"You're serious?" he asked. "You'll move in with me?"

"I will. If you'll have me."

"I want you with me. I can't tell you how happy that makes me. I promise you will have all the freedom you desire. I'm not trying to lock you down. I would never do that. We are going to support each other. It's all about us being a team in this life. I've got your back, and I know you have mine. I don't care what Austin tries to throw at you. I'm going to be there to volley it right back."

I felt like the luckiest woman alive. I had him in my corner, and that was all I needed. "Thank you. Thank you for being my rock and just being so damn good. I know the next few weeks and probably months are going to be a little rough. I am glad I have you in my corner. I know I can get through this with you by my side."

"Always," he said firmly. "I will always be right there beside you."

Chapter Twelve

Cooper

IT WAS WEIRD TO THINK I was only going to be going to her apartment a few more times. Then, whenever I wanted to see her, I just had to go home. We were going to live together. It was like I was stepping into a world I had only ever dreamed about. I found myself fantasizing about my future. Our future. It wasn't something I had ever allowed myself to do before.

When I got to her apartment, it looked like it had been ransacked. There were boxes everywhere. She and Piper were sitting in the middle of the living room floor. "Wow," I said as I looked around. "You have a lot of stuff."

"Are you changing your mind about letting me move in?" she asked with a laugh.

"Not a chance."

"Don't worry, I'm going to put most of it in storage."

"No way. You are moving in. All of you. We'll make room."

"Have I told you how sweet you are?"

"Yes, you have. What can I help with?"

"We should probably actually be packing, but we got a little distracted." She held up a large photo album. "Remember when I went through that scrapbooking phase?"

I groaned and moved around some boxes to take a seat on the couch. "When you were forced to take it as an elective because there was nothing else available? You complained about it for weeks."

"I complained, but then I loved it."

"Which era is that one from?"

Piper handed me the book. "This is freshman year."

It was the year I'd first met her. I opened the book and smiled at the first picture. It was a picture of the college sign with her standing next to it. The smile on her face was so her. "You're a baby," I said and touched the picture.

"I was. I look back now, and I can't believe that was ever me. I was wide-eyed and innocent."

"And then you met me," I teased.

"You corrupted me."

"I sure as hell tried."

Tatum pushed Piper. "It was her. She corrupted me. Remember when you took me to that frat party?"

"You had fun."

I listened to them reminisce while I flipped through the pages of the book. It was like watching her emerge from a cocoon. I remembered when I'd first seen her. I was older than her and probably shouldn't have set my sights on a woman three years younger, but it was like being struck by lightning.

"Look at this one," Piper said and handed me another album.

I opened it up, and the first picture in the album was of me and her. It was pre-Austin. "Wow," I said as I stared down at the picture. We both looked so young. I remembered the day the picture was taken. "This was the first day of spring break."

"Yep. We went to San Diego and stayed in that rental house with like ten people."

I laughed at the memory. "I don't think I slept that whole week."

"None of us did," Piper said with a laugh.

"That was a lot of fun," I said and turned the page. "I remember this picture."

"Which one?"

I turned the album to face them. Piper groaned. "I'm so wasted in that picture. Look at my eyes."

"Uh, I'm not exactly looking fresh as a daisy," Tatum said with a laugh. "Cooper was holding us both up. Remember we went down to the beach. It was like three o'clock in the morning. The police chased us out of there."

I shook my head. "When we got back to school, I don't think I left my bed for at least two days. That was the worst hangover of my life."

"We had so much fun though," Tatum said.

I put the album down and waited for the next one. "That's it?"

"I started dating Austin my sophomore year," she said with a sigh. "I didn't scrapbook anymore. I just have this." She held up a small box. I leaned forward to take it from her. When I opened it, I discovered it was mostly pictures of her and Austin.

"I think I should burn them."

I looked at her. "Why?"

"It feels wrong to take those pictures to your house."

"It's our house, and as much as I'd like to pretend he didn't exist, he did. He was a part of your life. Don't burn them on my account."

I pulled out a picture of me and her. Austin had taken the picture. That had been in the early days, before he tried to push me out of her life. "I like this picture. Can I keep it?"

I held it up for her to see. She smiled. "I love that picture. I'll have it framed."

I looked at the picture once again. I looked miserable. I had spent the day hanging out with her and Austin. I had been in love with her back then. After spending the day watching them hang on each other, I was jealous and felt like my soul had been crushed. Austin was every-thing I wasn't. I saw the way she looked at him and was convinced she would never look at me the same way. Back then, I never imagined I could have a woman like her.

I put the picture to the side and flipped through the others. "Here," I said and handed the box to Piper.

"I'll put the box in his pile," she said.

"Whose pile?"

"The Austin pile."

I glanced over at an opened box. "What's that?"

"His stuff," Tatum said. "I'm not sure what to do with it, but I don't want it. I don't want to see him to give it back, so for now, it goes in a box."

"I told her to burn it," Piper chimed in. "I read a book once about a group of ladies that did some ritual that involved burning her ex's things."

"I think that's called witchcraft," Tatum said.

"But how satisfying would it be?" Piper pointed out. "He gave you a signed copy of his book. You have to burn that."

I rolled my eyes. "I think it's better suited for the trash."

"Me too," Tatum agreed. "I'll throw it all in the trash."

"You don't think he might want some of that back?" I asked.

She shrugged. "I honestly don't care. I doubt it. If I have it, he's probably forgotten about it."

"But you're supposed to be the bigger person," Piper teased.

She rolled her eyes and tossed something at the box. "Fine, I'll have it delivered."

"I'd be happy to take it to him," I offered.

Piper burst into laughter. "I would pay to see that."

"My hero." Tatum fanned her face.

"I'll always be your hero."

"You know what, I'm starving," Piper said and got to her feet. "You guys in the mood for Thai?"

"I can order in," I offered.

"I'll go pick it up," she said. "I'll be back in about forty-five minutes. All right? Forty-five minutes."

She looked from me to Tatum and then back at me. I winked. "Got it."

"I like you, Cooper, but if I come back and see your willy, I'm not going to be happy."

I smiled and nodded. "Willy is not for your eyes."

"Good. The usual order?"

"Yes, please," Tatum said.

Piper left us alone. I immediately got up and pulled her up off the floor. I kissed her, running my hands through her hair. "I missed you."

"I missed you."

"How are you feeling about all of this?"

"I'm good. I'm not the least bit freaked out. The timing was actually very good. My lease is up in a month. Rent is due in two weeks. My deposit will cover the last month, and I'm out of it. I guess there is always a silver lining if you look hard enough."

I smiled, my arms wrapping around her waist as I stared into her eyes. "I'm glad you can see the silver lining. I certainly see it. I'm very sorry you lost your job, but I can't feel that badly about it. It brought you into my arms and my bed. Our bed. We get to start this whole new chapter together."

"I'm looking forward to it. I really am."

"I'll spend this weekend cleaning out the garage. I'll move my exercise equipment out there and we can use the spare room for your stuff. Although I don't want it to be your stuff and my stuff. We'll mingle it all together."

She giggled. "Aren't I supposed to be the one who does the nesting?"

"I can't help it. I can't wait to come home after work and right into your arms. We get to be old and boring together. Eat grilled chicken for dinner and watch reruns of Friends. We don't have to go out anywhere or do anything except be together."

"You sound like we are retiring from the world."

"I wouldn't mind doing exactly that if I got to spend all my time with you."

"Damn," she whispered. "You know you are one smooth talker. You can make a girl dream big."

"I dream big every time I see you."

I kissed her again, infusing the kiss with all the happiness I felt about her moving in with me. The kiss heated up as it usually did. I didn't think I would ever grow tired of being with her. Every time I was with her, it was like it was the first time. I discovered new spots on her body that could leave her trembling.

"I want you," she breathed.

"I'm not going anywhere."

I slid my hands down her hips and thighs and then grabbed her ass. I jerked her against me and held her close. Things were just about to get really good when I heard the door open followed by Piper's groan. "Ew. I told you I didn't want to see any willies."

"My willy is not visible," I said and turned around.

"You guys are worse than dogs in heat."

"You left us alone," Tatum said with a laugh.

"Let's eat and then get back to work," Piper said and put the bags on the table. "I'm starving."

We all dug in, swapping boxes and dishing up like we had done so many times over the years. Some people assumed I was gay for the longest time because my two best friends were girls. Beautiful women with boyfriends. I didn't care about the gossip. I only cared about hanging out with her.

"This is going to be so much easier once you two live together," Piper said. "I'll be able to crash your house, and you'll both be there. We won't have to call and coordinate. We won't have a scrunchy-faced dude constantly scrutinizing everything we say and do. We won't have to keep it down because he is writing. Seriously, writing? What was he doing in there? Beating off? Looking at porn? We all know that he wasn't actually writing."

"I'm sure he was in there sexting with his flavor of the week," Tatum scoffed. "I'm just glad I don't have to worry about it anymore."

"Me too," I muttered.

"We'll have to have a housewarming party," Piper said.

"A party?" I questioned.

"Well, not like a rager, but you know."

I looked to Tatum to judge her reaction. "What do you think?"

"I think having a few people over once we get settled could be fun."

"Then we will have a party," I said.

It was the only thing they needed to hear. While I stuffed my face, they planned the party that wasn't really a party. I missed these moments. I missed the three of us getting to hang out. The last year or so, things had been strained. Austin had pretty much forbidden her to hang out with us. We were all back together. It was like a clou had been lifted. I only wished that cloud had been lifted earlier. We needed to make up for lost time.

Chapter Thirteen

Tatum

"ARGH!" I GROANED AND walked out of the bedroom. I couldn't do it anymore. "When in the hell did I collect so much shit?"

I felt like I'd been packing for weeks. It was one box after another after another. It felt like it was never going to end. I'd already made a rather large donation to the local shelter, and I still had too much shit. No wonder my credit cards were so full. I never saw it before until now. Now that I was trying to pack it all into boxes, it seemed like every time I closed the closet door, it multiplied.

"I can't. I can't do it."

I grabbed my purse and left. I showed up at Piper's and pounded on the door, but she didn't answer. I used my spare key to open her door. I knew she was home. She was likely buried in her work. When she was on a roll, she never answered the door or her phone.

I could hear the usual classical music she listened to when she was working. It was her mojo, she claimed. I thought it was annoying as hell, but it helped her. At least that's what she said. I carefully walked to her extra bedroom that doubled as her office and peeked inside. Sure enough, she was tapping away on the keyboard. Her fingers flew across the keys. I could see the red squiggly lines from the door. That was how she worked. She didn't bother with the editing when she was in the zone.

I walked away and opened her fridge. "Damn," I whispered. The woman had almost no food in her fridge. Again, another sign of her in the zone.

I found some bread and made a couple of sandwiches. I didn't bother her but waited for her to come up for air. She came out of the bedroom looking a little wild. Her short hair was a mess, her eyes a little bugged out.

"How long have you been in there?"

"What time is it?"

"Just after four."

She grimaced. "I should pee."

"What?"

"I started around seven this morning. I don't think I've peed."

"Go pee. I made you a sandwich and I'll get you a glass of water. You're probably dehydrated. You have to remember to eat and drink when you go on one of these little frenzies."

The girl needed a babysitter. I filled her a glass with ice and water and waited. When she returned, her hair had been combed and her face washed. "Thanks," she said and took a very manly bite of the sandwich. "What brings you by?"

"I was going out of my mind with the packing. I remembered I hate moving. I'm seriously considering just leaving everything and starting over from scratch."

She laughed. "The accumulation is no joke. I don't think I'm ever moving, and if I do, I'm going to pay someone to pack for me."

"It would be worth it."

"Will you do me a favor?" she asked.

"Sure."

"Will you edit the first half of my book?"

"I thought you didn't want me to read it."

"I didn't, but now I do. I need someone to make sure I'm on the right track. I feel like I am, but I need someone I trust. You are the only one I trust."

"I don't know. Editors can be pretty territorial. I don't want to play in someone else's sandbox. My style is not going to match your editor's style. I don't want you to get in trouble."

She snorted. "It's my book. I can let anyone I want read it and edit it."

"You know what I mean."

"This is my last book with them. Once I turn this in, my contract is fulfilled. I'm going to be looking for a new publisher, and I want you to be my editor."

"Sweetie, I am jobless."

"Not if you are my editor."

"You can't afford to pay me."

She burst into laughter. "Someone is very high on themselves."

"You know what I mean."

"Do it as a friend, please? I need your opinion. This book is a little different for me. I feel like I am stepping out of my comfort zone in a big way. I need you to cheer me on or make me stop before I make a total fool of myself."

I laughed. "All right, I would love to."

"Thank you."

"How's it going with Vance?" I asked her as she scarfed down the second sandwich.

She bobbed her head back and forth. "I'm not sure."

"What do you mean?"

"We've talked a few times, but we haven't gone out again. I told him I was too busy."

"Why? You guys got along so well, and he seemed like a really nice guy."

"I don't know. I'm in the middle of my book, and I can't afford any distractions right now."

I rolled my eyes. "I would think hooking up with this guy would help inspire you. He's hot, like really hot. That's the kind of guy ladies write about."

"I don't know. Maybe the timing isn't right."

I studied her for several seconds. "What's really going on?"

"I don't want to start this thing off on a lie or with me being shady."

"Why would you lie or be shady?"

"Because you told him I would tell him the long story about you and Austin."

I waved a hand. "The guy does not care about that. He isn't going to ask."

"But what if he does? Am I supposed to lie? Am I supposed to tell him it's none of his business? I do like him, but I don't want this to start off on the wrong foot. If I'm holding back or he thinks I don't trust him enough to tell him a simple story, he's going to do the same. I don't want that kind of relationship anymore. I want the real thing. I want him to want to tell me all about his day. I want him to feel like he can tell me about the asshole at work that took the last bit of coffee and didn't make more."

I took a moment to digest all the information. "Wow."

"I know I sound ridiculous, but I want what you and Cooper have. You can tell him anything, and he knows you will. He tells you about his day and so on. That's how that tight bond develops. I can't tell Vance much of anything. I'm not sorry to say, but you and Cooper are kind of my life. I don't get out much. I don't have a lot to talk about. Your thing right now is what is important in my life. I can't tell him about that, which means I have nothing to say, and he's going to know I am holding back."

I held up a hand. "Okay, overthink much? Woman, take a beat. You are going just a little crazy worrying about something that isn't even a thing."

"But it could be a thing."

"Why?"

"I can't go blabbing about this whole stolen book thing. Not yet."

I grabbed her hand, mostly to get her to take a breath. "Yes, you can. It's going to be out soon enough anyway. I'm already fired. The lawyer is already aware of the situation. The only person you are protecting is Austin."

"But wouldn't I be breaking some confidentiality laws?"

"I don't see how, but you could speak in hypotheticals if that makes you feel better. It's up to you if you want to tell him, but don't think you have to hold back and protect me. I'm fine with it. It's going to get out there eventually. I know Austin and his cohorts are going to be very busy smearing my name. At least this way I might have one ally. Assuming he even cares. This is our very small world. I'm sure he has much bigger things to worry about than some no-name editor and a flash in the pan writer that's going nowhere."

"True," she agreed. "I don't know. We'll see. I've probably missed my chance. I've been putting him off for days."

"I saw the way he looked at you. I think you've still got a very good chance."

She smiled. "I hope so. What about you?"

"No, you don't have a chance with me."

She laughed. "How are you feeling about the big move? You know you are welcome to move in with me. I know this is a huge step. You never lived with Austin, and you were with him for years."

"Austin was different. I probably would have moved in with him if he would have let me. I'm glad I didn't."

"But do you want to move in with Cooper or is this out of necessity?"

"I told him no at first, but then I got to thinking about it, and I realized I did want to. I do want to spend my life with him, and we would have moved in eventually. I'm sure of that. I am leaping with both feet. All or nothing. If things fall apart, so be it. At least I will have known I wasn't afraid to step outside my comfort level. I really think it's the right thing to do."

She was smiling. "Good. That's what I needed to hear."

"What do you mean?"

"Because I needed to know if you were truly serious about this or if you were just doing it because it was your only option. Now, in a month or a year if you come to me and blame me for not talking you out of it, I'll remind you of this conversation."

"I don't think that's going to happen," I said with a laugh. "But thanks for the vote of confidence."

"I'm just looking out for your best interest. I think it's going to be fine. I'm excited for you guys. It's like we've all been waiting for this for years. It's finally happening."

I let out a happy sigh. "I know. I'm so looking forward to the future with him."

"All right, all right, now you're just getting sappy. I'm going to put the book on a thumb drive and then I am getting back to work."

She disappeared and returned a minute later. "Be brutally honest," she said as she handed it to me.

"Of course. I'll talk to you later. If I don't hear from you, I'll come by in the morning and make sure you haven't seized up at the computer."

"That would be funny if it wasn't true," she said with a small laugh.

I left her place, feeling rejuvenated and ready to get back to the packing. When I got home, there was a note stapled to my door. "We will find you," I read aloud.

I looked around to see if the culprit was still around. The hairs on the back of my neck stood up, and a cold chill raced down my spine.

Chapter Fourteen

Cooper

I WHIPPED INTO THE parking lot of her apartment complex and barely got the engine turned off before I was out the door and racing upstairs. I burst into her apartment. My heart was pounding in my chest with sweat dripping down my back. She was sitting at her dining table with a single piece of paper on the table in front of her.

"Are you okay?" I asked and rushed to her side.

"I'm fine."

I snatched the paper up and read the message. "What the fuck? What is his game?"

"Whose game?"

"You know who! This is Austin!"

She sighed and slowly nodded. "It probably is, but I could never prove it."

"Who else would leave a threatening note on your door? He's a fucking coward and can't say it to your face."

"I'm sure it was him, but how am I going to prove it? It could have just been a silly prank. It could have been left on the wrong door."

I stared at her. "Really? You think that is what happened here? Austin threatened you. He attempted to threaten me. I have no doubt in my mind this is him."

She slowly nodded. "I know. I'm sure it was him or someone working on his behalf."

"I'm going to kill the son of a bitch," I growled.

"You can't do that because then you'd go to prison. I've read and edited a lot of mystery novels. Neither of us is capable of covering up that kind of a crime."

"No body, no crime," I replied.

She smiled. "Where would said body possibly go? There is always evidence. A hair. A fiber. Always something. I can't have your pretty face in prison. You would be someone's bitch, and I don't like to share."

I smirked. "I don't think I'd last in prison, which would motivate me to be smart. Dexter got away with it."

"Until he didn't."

"You'd be there to help me clean things up."

She slowly shook her head. "I don't like blood."

"Poison."

"Then they would point the finger at me. Don't you know women are more likely to use poison to commit murder?"

"What? Why?"

"Because women don't like messy."

"Huh, it's just a little scary that you know that," I told her. "I'll just have to make sure I don't get caught."

"You'll miss something."

"Thanks for the confidence."

She laughed. "You are upset that I'm not confident you can get away with murder."

The absurdity of it was kind of funny. "I would kill him for you."

"Then I'd have to read books on prison breaks. I would have to bust you out of there."

"How would you do it? Sneak a file in a cake?"

She made a raspberry face. "Shoot, that's for amateurs. I'd be more like flirting with a guard and planting some explosives on the bars and blasting you out of there."

"How much flirting with the guard would you do? Would you flash them? Show them a little skin?"

She pretended to think about it. "I might have a little nip slip. Totally by accident. It would be just enough to disarm them."

"You'd flash your nipple for me?"

"I sure would. I might even flash full boob if that's what it took."

I had to laugh. I pulled her up and into my arms. "I'll keep that in mind. I'm not sure I want you flashing your boobs. I kind of like the idea that only I get to see them."

"I could flash some leg, but from personal experience, it's the magic of the nipple. Men are suckers for a boob."

"We are programmed that way," I laughed. "I especially love these boobs." I cupped her breast and gently squeezed. I was glad we were able to laugh at a time when I didn't feel like laughing at all. I was furious. I really did want to make that piece of shit pay. He deserved to rot in jail.

She wrapped her arms around me and hugged me close. "Thank you for coming. I hope I didn't freak you out too badly."

"No. Yes. I was freaked out, but I'm glad you are okay. I don't want to think what could have happened if you were here."

"It was a note. I don't think the person that left it meant to do anything. It's a coward's way to deliver a threat."

"Yes, it is," she agreed. "I'm sure it was him. He's throwing a tantrum. He knows he's screwed, and this is his way of trying to fight back. We both know he's going down."

"I don't like the idea of him wanting to come after you," I told her. "I don't like it at all. I'm glad you are moving in. I'll sleep much better at night knowing I'm with you."

She leaned back before giving me a quick kiss on the lips. "I appreciate that. Now that the initial shock is over, I feel kind of silly. I overreacted. It was just a note. Not even a threatening note really. They'll find me? Seriously, they left the note on my front door. I think it's kind of a given they found me."

"It's still risky. We don't know how pissed he's going to be when the full weight of the situation slaps him upside the head. He is going to lose everything. His name is going to be ruined. His career is going to be ruined. I think you need to expect him to want revenge."

"I'm sure he'll want revenge. He's already trying to get it by having me fired. There's nothing more he can do. He ruined my reputation and will probably slander me to anyone that will listen."

"I worry you might not be safe."

She smiled and put her hand on my cheek. "I appreciate the thought, but I don't think Austin is capable of violence. That would get him dirty and require exertion. He's not about to break into a sweat for me."

"I'm serious," I told her. "What do you think about a security detail?"

She laughed and then quickly stopped when she saw I was serious. "What are you talking about?"

"Someone to keep an eye on things."

"On me?"

"On you. Your apartment. Another set of eyes. Someone that could take pictures to prove it's Austin making the threats."

"You mean a private investigator?"

"I mean both."

"Cooper, no. That is not necessary. This was a single note. I don't need a babysitter or a spy. This isn't that dangerous."

"Isn't it? You're taking away a man's livelihood. You're taking away the one thing he wanted most in the world."

She smirked. "Two things really. Money and fame. He wanted those two things over everything else."

"Exactly! He's going to try and stop you. He's going to want to make sure you can't take those things from him!"

"Relax, Cooper. Austin is a lot of things, but he's not violent."

"He's going to want that recording back."

She nodded. "Yes, I know. I've made a copy, and I've hidden both copies in separate places. He's not going to get them."

"I may have already contacted someone," I said without looking her in the eye.

"You did what?"

"I was terrified when you called me. I train a guy that runs a security firm. He's willing to jump into this as a personal favor."

"You did what!" she shrieked. "How much is that going to cost?"

"I've got it handled."

"No! Dammit, no! You don't get to *handle* this. This is my life."

"Tatum, I care about you, and I'm worried Austin is going to try something. He might hurt you. I can't let that happen."

"So instead of murdering him and going to prison, you're imprisoning me? How is that fair?"

"I'm not imprisoning you. I'm making sure you are safe. I'm making sure your evidence is safe. If it is Austin and he comes back, the PI will get it on tape. It will be more evidence against him. He'll get criminal charges pressed against him if he tries to hurt you or intimidate you in any way."

"No. Dammit, Cooper. Why would you do that? Why even ask me if you've already made that decision for me?"

"Because I knew you would be worried about cost. I've got it covered. I give him some free sessions and he does this for me."

She shook her head and stepped away from me. "This is exactly what I was afraid of."

"What were you afraid of?"

"You taking over my life. You deciding what was best for me. I'm not a child. I am not an idiot. I'm not trying to get killed, but I know Austin a lot better than you do. This is way over the top. This is too much. You don't get to decide this stuff for me."

"I'm not taking over your life. I'm just trying to keep you safe."

She was glaring at me. I was in trouble. I had expected a little push back, but I never expected her to be this pissed. "Then you should have talked to me before you went off and made a decision about my life. My life, Cooper. I told you I wanted my freedom. I don't want to lose myself. You have always been like this."

"Like this?" I asked. I was sure I was supposed to be offended. I just wasn't sure why.

"Yes, overprotective. You are always so worried I'm making mistakes. You are three years older than I am. Three years! That doesn't exactly make you my elder. You are no wiser than I am."

I held up a hand. "Calm down. You are going off the deep end about nothing. I did this because I care about you. I love you, and I don't want to see you hurt. You've always had a blind spot when it comes to Austin. He's bad news. I do not trust him not to lose his shit and try to hurt you. If not him, someone he hires. It isn't just Austin you've fucked with. The publishing company is threatened as well. Gary Simms stands to lose a lot if this whole scandal makes the news. You don't think he might want to keep you quiet?"

"You've been watching way too much TV," she scoffed. "This isn't twenty-twenty. This is real life, and people like Gary and Austin don't do murder for hire, and they certainly don't do it themselves."

"Do you know that for sure?"

"Do you?" she shot back.

"Look, you're upset. It's been a rough few weeks. Let's go home. We'll have some dinner and a glass of wine."

"No."

"What?"

"No. I'm staying here tonight."

I threw my hands up. "Fine. I've got my bag from the other night in the truck."

"No," she said again. "I'm staying here alone. I need to be alone. I need to think."

"Think about what?"

"This. All of it. You invading my privacy and stomping all over my freedom."

She was being dramatic. I wasn't going to change my mind, and standing in front of her and arguing was only going to lead to some hurt feelings. It was best to walk away before something was said. Something that couldn't be taken back.

"Fine, I'll leave. Lock the fucking door and call me if you want to talk."

"Duh!" she called out.

I paused at the door and very angrily said, "I love you."

"Love you too," she shot back as if she was telling me to go to hell.

I slammed the door and waited. When I didn't hear the lock turn, I opened it again. "I said to lock the damn door!"

She stomped toward me and slammed the door in my face. I heard the lock turn followed by her slapping the door. "Happy now?" she shouted through the door.

"Yes!"

I stomped downstairs and got into my truck. Damn if the woman didn't piss me off something fierce!

Chapter Fifteen

Tatum

HINDSIGHT GAVE ME A lot more than twenty-twenty vision. It also gave me the added luxury of being humiliated by my behavior last night. I still couldn't believe how I'd acted. I could come up with about a hundred excuses, but I doubted any of them were really valid.

I was embarrassed by my outburst. I just wasn't sure how I was going to fix it. I felt like our entire relationship had been me apologizing to him. How many times was the guy going to forgive me? I needed to say it again. I was such a fool. Last night had been nothing more than a reaction to a horrible situation. I'd taken out my frustration on the wrong guy.

I showered and pulled on one of the shirts he'd left at my place. With the way things were going, it might be the last thing I got from him. I made a cup of coffee and sat down with my laptop to start going over Piper's book.

"Wow," I said aloud as I read through the first chapter. "Damn, Piper."

I grabbed my phone and sent her a quick text to let her know how much I loved the book. I loved it so much I was certain it was her best work yet. She didn't answer, which didn't surprise me. She was proba-bly writing again.

There was a knock on the door. My heart leapt into my throat. I scanned the area looking for a weapon of some sort. I hopped up from the chair and grabbed a knife from the counter. With my heart pounding in my chest, I started toward the door. When the handle started to turn, I almost puked. I held the knife up. I wasn't sure I could stab someone, but I was going to try.

"Tatum?" I heard Cooper call out.

The door opened all the way, and he stepped inside carrying a tray of coffee and a bag from my favorite doughnut shop. "Cooper." I breathed his name.

He looked at me and then the knife in my hand. "Are you okay?"

"I thought you were breaking in."

"You were going to stab me with a butter knife?"

I looked at the knife in my hand. I hadn't even realized it was a butter knife. I was definitely not going to be saving myself or anyone else. "Oh."

"Did something happen?"

"No. Nothing. You just startled me."

"I can see that. I brought you an apology breakfast."

"I owe you the apology breakfast."

He locked the door and put the goodies on the table. "I'm sorry I overstepped the boundaries of our relationship. I was panicked and could only think about protecting you."

We sat down at the table. I grabbed one of the doughnuts and took a bite. "I was a little more worried than I let on. I shouldn't have taken my fear out on you."

"I think we were both a little afraid."

"A lot."

He smirked. "A lot."

"A PI is a good idea. I don't necessarily want a security guard, but if your guy is willing to keep an eye on Austin, I would appreciate it. I don't want him on me, but if Austin comes after me or tries to threaten me, I want proof of it."

He nodded. "That works for me. You have to promise me you'll be aware of your surroundings. Don't stare at your phone when you're walking or get caught up in a conversation. Keep your eyes open when I'm not with you."

"I can do that."

"I'm sorry I overstepped," he said again. "I can't tell you how worried I was. I was so worried you were going to be hurt. I got a little crazy."

"I get it. I do. It's actually kind of sweet that you cared so much."

He reached across the table and grabbed my hand. "I care a lot."

"I'm sorry."

"Don't be."

"Do you have to get to work?" I asked him.

He slowly shook his head. "Not for a while."

"I think I'd like a makeup kiss," I said and got up from the chair.

"I like that shirt," he said with a grin.

"You should. It's yours."

"I know."

He grabbed me and pulled me close. I straddled him on the chair. His hand reached up, sliding into my hair and pulling my face to his. I kissed him in an attempt to make up for the craziness yesterday. His hand pulled my hair, jerking my head back and exposing my neck to his mouth. His mouth was hot and furious as he pulled the shirt down to give him access to my collarbone.

"I have to have you," he growled and rose to his feet. He hoisted me up and carried me to the bedroom.

He very unceremoniously dropped me on the mattress before he started to rip off his clothes. I pulled his shirt over my head, sitting on the edge of the bed and waiting for him. He lunged for me, knocking me onto my back on the bed. He kissed me like a starving man. I wanted to ravage him. I used my body weight to roll him off me and onto his back.

"I am going to have you," I told him as I straddled him.

I ran my hands down his chest, squeezing his pecs before bending forward to kiss him. His hands reached for my breasts, squeezing and pulling before pinching my nipples. My head jerked away from his as I cried out. I rose up, thrusting my breasts forward and arching my back as my nails dug into his flesh.

He roared and used his abs to sit up. His mouth covered one nipple. He sucked it hard into his mouth while his hands worked into my hair and pulled my head back further. A cry escaped my throat. I dropped my head forward and pulled his hair. His head jerked back with his mouth open. I covered his mouth with my own and plunged my tongue inside.

When his mouth pulled away from mine, I felt like I'd been left empty. I pushed him back. He lay on his back with his arms spread wide. "Damn," I murmured. "Have I ever told you how sexy you are?"

He grinned. "Maybe, but feel free to say it again."

I leaned forward and kissed his chest. My tongue swirled around his nipple before sliding over to the other one. His hands slowly slid up and down my back. Then I bit him. He sucked in a breath through his teeth, and the gentle caress up and down my back turned far more intense.

He rose up, throwing me off him and turning the tables with him on top of me. The frustration from last night bubbled into passion. I opened my legs to him, demanding he take me. His cock rubbed against my pussy. My panties were damp. I was so ready for him.

He growled and reached between us. "Fuck," he muttered when he encountered my panties.

I struggled under him. I wanted them off. He grabbed a fistful of the satin fabric and jerked. My ass lifted off the bed with the force. He jerked again, and I heard the fabric tear. In a split second he was pushing inside me.

I moaned, taking every last inch of him. He was breathing hard, gasping as he went completely still inside me. "Holy shit," he breathed.

"Ride me," I whispered.

"Baby, I'm barely keeping it together."

"Don't keep anything together. Take me."

He moved inside me slowly at first before he gave over to the passion that had been burning inside us since last night. "I like fighting with you," he grunted.

"Me too."

He pulled out of me and flipped me over to my stomach. I lay flat on my stomach with my arms stretched out straight over my head. I grabbed the edge of the mattress while he penetrated me once again.

"So good," he hissed before he picked up the pace once again.

His body slapped against mine. The sound of our passion bubbling over fueled the fire inside me. I held on for dear life while he took me to new heights. I felt the orgasm rising. "Cooper, I'm so close."

"I feel it. Hold on baby. Hold on to something."

I understood the warning. The power humming through his body and into mine was amazing. It fueled the passion in a way I had never experienced before. When the orgasm hit, I had to shout. The combination of his lust mixing with my own made me dizzy. He shouted as he came inside me. Solid, hard thrusts pushed me to the edge of the bed. When he collapsed on top of me, the balance of weight shifted, and we fell headfirst over the side.

I screamed before bursting into laughter.

"Are you okay?" he asked as he scrambled to get off me.

I was still laughing. "Yes. I'm fine. I'm better than fine."

"Shit. Sorry. I got carried away."

I grabbed his face with my hands. "Me too, in the best way possible."

He got to his feet and helped me up. "I want to do this again."

I smiled and rubbed my body against his. "I would like that."

He reached down and grabbed my ass. He jerked me against his body. "Woman, I'm going to do this every night. Every morning. Every fucking chance I get. I want to bury myself inside you and never come up for air."

"What about work?" I whispered against his lips.

"Fuck work. I want to stay right here with you."

As good as that sounded, I knew it wasn't possible. "You're the breadwinner," I reminded him. "You can't stay."

"But I want to," he groaned. His forehead rested against mine as we stood skin to skin. "I want nothing more than to stay here with you."

"I'll see you tonight."

"Are you kicking me out?" he pouted.

"No, but you do need to go to work, and I need to finish packing."

He sighed and kissed me hard before pulling away. "Fine, but I do this under protest."

"Your protest is noted."

I pulled on his shirt, not bothering with panties. I needed to find panties. The packing had completely disrupted everything in my life. With a great deal of struggle and resistance, I managed to get him out the door and on his way to work. I had a feeling this was going to be the way things were when we lived together. There were going to be a lot of late mornings.

I couldn't be the least bit upset about the thought of making him late for work.

Chapter Sixteen

Cooper

I DRIFTED AROUND THE gym. It was a slow day. People tended to come in waves. Right now, there was a lull. I did a little cleaning and a lot of daydreaming. I thought a lot about Austin and what he was doing to Tatum. I didn't like it, but I couldn't exactly put a stop to it. Not yet. I needed him to dig his hole a little deeper.

Damon was sitting on a weight bench with his phone in hand. At least I was trying to look busy. "Are you doing anything after work tonight?" I asked him.

He shrugged. "That depends."

"On?"

"What is it you want me to do?"

"Help me move Tatum into my house."

He groaned and made a big fuss. "How much shit does she have?"

"Not much. We've moved a lot of the boxes, but there are some heavy things."

He sighed. "Fine. I guess. You're going to guilt me into it."

"Very funny. I'll owe you one."

"Yes, you will. Things are still going well between you?"

"Yep."

"That has to be some kind of a record," he joked.

I thought it best not to tell him about the little fight we'd had last week. "I think things are going to be much better. Once she moves in with me, we'll have to work through our fights."

"She can't run away from you."

I winked. "Nope."

"All right, I'll be there."

"I should probably warn you about something."

He raised his eyebrows. "I'm afraid to ask."

"Austin is a dick."

"I thought we already knew that."

"No, I mean he threatened her."

His face grew hard. "What the hell do you mean he threatened her?"

"There was a note on her door. I know it was him. I don't trust him not to pull something. I've got a PI digging into him and his background. She refused to let me hire security for her. The PI is keeping an eye on Austin, and if he goes anywhere near her, I'll know about it."

"Damn, all because she busted him cheating?"

Damon knew the rough version of the story. I didn't want to get into all the dirty details with him. "His image is about to get tarnished. He doesn't like the idea of losing his fame and money."

"Understandable."

"What's the PI after?" he asked.

I was about to tell him when my phone rang. I checked the screen and saw it was the PI. "Alan," I greeted him. "Is everything okay?"

"Yes and no. Tatum is fine."

Relief flooded me. "Thank goodness."

"I've been digging into the publishing company," he said.

"And?"

"It goes a lot deeper than you thought."

"How so?"

"There are very few authors that are producing original content. Most of it is hijacked."

"What?"

"Yep. I can't tell you how I know, but we may have read a few files with NDAs. Upon doing a little more digging, we discovered there are numerous authors that have signed away the rights to their books. Some of them have ghostwriting contracts, but the bulk of them signed the confidentiality clauses for a single book. We did a little more digging and managed to find those books had already been self-published. Some were available for just a few short months before being jerked down, and others had been on various websites for years."

"No shit?" I was surprised. Shocked that it was more than just Austin. I had met a few of the authors that had contracts with the company. I couldn't believe it was all lies.

"Yes. There are a few legitimate authors on the payroll."

"Is Piper Osborne one?" I asked. I knew the truth, but I had to confirm it.

"She is legitimate. According to some of the emails we saw, Miss Osborne is terminating her contract after she publishes a book she is currently working on. They are trying to persuade her to stay, but it sounds like her mind is made up."

"Good," I said. "What else?"

"There is something else, but I don't want to say anything until I get more details."

"What is it?"

"There is an email chain between a few of the management staff. The emails didn't make sense until we started reading between the lines. It's something I've seen before."

"What have you seen?"

"It could just be a book plot, but it seems like they are talking about a kidnapping."

"A what? Kidnapping? What the hell are you talking about?"

"Don't worry. I've got her covered. I don't know if it's what I suspect. They've never used the word kidnapping. They could be talking about something else. I've got my assistant digging through the emails."

"Send me what you have. I need all the evidence I can get to nail this bastard."

He blew out a breath. "Some of it can be used as evidence, but there are some things that weren't entirely legally obtained. We need to be careful. If we are caught breaking the law, it isn't going to do you any good in court."

"I understand. Whatever you can get me, I would appreciate it."

"I'll call you tomorrow with an update."

"Thank you."

I ended the call and couldn't shake the feeling of dread. "What was that about?" Damon asked.

I shook my head. "I'm not entirely sure. The PI found dirt on the publishing company, but so far, Austin might get out of it. He didn't write the checks, and he can easily claim they made him put his name on the books. I need more."

"What were you saying about kidnapping? That sounds ominous."

"I'm not sure. He said they picked up on some emails that seemed to be alluding to kidnapping, but he couldn't say for sure."

"You think they want to kidnap Tatum?"

"No. I don't know. It definitely makes me worried. Hopefully this is all over tomorrow."

"What happens tomorrow?"

"She will turn over her evidence to an attorney for the authors. Then it will be up to them to do something about it."

"But she's a witness," he reminded me. "She's still a threat to them."

"Thanks for that. Just what I needed to hear."

"I'm only saying you need to keep a close eye on her."

"I am. I will."

"Are you going to tell her?"

I looked out the window, staring at the people walking around without a care in the world. They were going about their day like it was no big deal to be alive without fear of being kidnapped. They were talking on their phones or focused on their destination. They weren't thinking about when someone might snatch them off the street. They were doing what people did.

"I don't know," I finally said.

"You don't think she has a right to know?"

"There might not be anything to know. It could be nothing. It might have nothing to do with her. I don't want to worry her if I don't have to. I don't want her to have to look over her shoulder or live in fear. That's no way to live. It isn't fair to her. She's already nervous after the note on her door. I don't want to make it worse for her. He wins if he takes away her sense of security."

He slowly nodded. "I get it, but if this is real, she needs to know she might be in danger. She can carry pepper spray. She needs to be able to defend herself."

I cringed at the thought of her having to fight off an attacker. That was not how I wanted to think of her spending her days. "I'll think about it. First, I'll see what the PI finds out. I'm not going to freak her out if there is nothing to worry about."

"But what if there *is* something to worry about?"

I rubbed a hand over my face. I didn't want to think about that. I couldn't. It made me crazy with fear and anger. "I'll think about it. She's going to be with me soon enough. I'll keep her safe."

"I have no doubt in my mind you'll walk through hell to keep her safe. Where is she now?"

"She's finishing packing. At least I hope she's finishing. She's been packing for days. I haven't seen any real progress. I'm so glad she started two weeks ago. It has not been a very quick process."

He laughed. "Having second thoughts about her moving in?"

"No, definitely not. It's crazy. I've been to her apartment several times. A hundred times. I never saw any of this stuff she keeps packing. It's like every time I go back, the boxes multiply, and there is still stuff that needs to be packed."

"You haven't had to move in a while," he said. "Trust me, it happens to the best of us. You never realize how much shit you have until it comes time to move. Are you going to have room at your place? You don't exactly live in a mansion."

I cringed. "My gym is now in the garage."

"Ouch. That had to have hurt."

"It's fine. I want her more than I want a weight bench."

"Maybe you guys should look for a bigger place," he suggested.

"She doesn't have a job right now."

"Oh, that's right. How's that going?"

"Austin has made sure she can't get a job as an editor. We're both hoping that once this whole scheme comes out, the other publishing houses will see she was the injured party. She had a stellar reputation before all of this. I just hope she gets it back. She loves what she does."

"It sucks she got taken down with this thing. That guy is such a piece of work."

I scoffed. "I cannot wait to see him knocked down a few pegs. I just wish I could be the one to push his ass off the pedestal he put himself on."

"You get a front row seat for when he does fall," he reminded me.

I grinned and nodded. "Damn straight. It's a day I have waited a long time for."

"What time should I be at her place?"

We talked about the plans for the night before it was time to get back to work. I was worried about Tatum. I didn't believe Austin had the balls to do anything to her. But Gary, that worried me. I considered calling Jill to get an idea of how much Gary knew. She had not been into the gym or shown up for her training sessions since Tatum had been fired. That told me she knew. She knew what her husband was up to and maybe even had a hand in it.

I felt like I could trust no one. That wasn't entirely true. I did trust Piper and Damon. Beyond them, I felt like anybody could be involved. Maybe I had watched too many movies. The Simms were connected. They had money and would not be happy to lose their revenue stream. Would they resort to kidnapping?

To what end?

My head was a mess. I had no idea what the hell was going on. My imagination was running wild. I had to take a step back and be rational. This was real life. This was not one of Austin's stories. This wasn't a television show.

"She's fine," I told myself. "She'll be fine."

She would be in my arms tonight. I would keep her safe. Which reminded me. I grabbed my keys and wallet and went out to find Damon. "I'm out of here," I told him.

"Already?"

"Look around, you don't need me here. I've got some errands to run."

"I'll see you in a bit."

I left the gym and headed for Home Depot. She was not going to appreciate the extra security measures, but I was going to protect the most precious thing in my life. I picked up new deadbolts, a chain lock, and a few security cameras. Those were going to be hard to get her to agree to, but they were going up. If Austin came around, I was going to make damn sure I had evidence to support the restraining order I slapped on him.

I had just enough time to get home and change out the deadbolts and install the chain on the front door. I was hoping she wouldn't notice the changes. It would be subtle. If she thought I was locking her down, she was going to run away screaming. I couldn't make her feel like she was in a gilded cage.

Chapter Seventeen

Tatum

I PUSHED THE BOX OF clothes across the floor and left it by the door with the others. I looked around my apartment. It was finally looking like I was moving. It had been one hell of a long process to get to this point.

My phone vibrated on the table. I considered ignoring it. "Your phone!" Piper called out from the bedroom where she was packing another box of stuff from my closet.

"It's probably just another prank call."

"I told you to block the number."

"I can't. It's private."

"You need to change your number," she hollered.

"It's probably just some punk kids. If I stop answering, they'll eventually get bored and give up."

She came out of the room and looked at me. "You've been saying that for days. They haven't stopped yet."

"I know."

"Do they ever say anything?"

"Nope. I don't even hear them breathing. Nothing. Just dead air."

"Creepy."

"No kidding. I cannot wait to move in with Cooper. I've tried to tell him I'm not freaked out, but it's starting to get to me. The note. The phone calls. I always feel like I'm being watched. I keep looking over my shoulder. I've started keeping my blinds closed. It's very creepy to think someone is out there."

She snorted. "Not someone—Austin. Austin is probably trying to intimidate you. Don't let him win."

"I know. I keep telling myself that, but it's still very creepy."

"Have you told him?" she asked.

I shook my head. "No. He's already anxious. I don't want him worrying any more than he has to. I want him to be able to relax."

She snorted. "As if that's ever going to happen. Cooper treats you like a fragile doll."

"He cares about me."

"Yes, he does, which is why you should tell him before he finds out. He's going to be hurt you didn't tell him. Then he's going to be pissed. He's going to go all caveman and he really is going to hire a security guard."

"I'll tell him after I'm in his house and all settled."

"I think you are walking a very dangerous line."

"I know, I know, but there is so much going on right now. We'll meet with the lawyer tomorrow, and then I can finally start moving forward. I can start looking for a job. I can finally say goodbye to Austin once and for all. He will not be my problem anymore."

"We can only hope."

"What about your book?" I asked her. "What happens if the company goes bankrupt before your book hits the presses?"

"I have my own lawyer looking into that. I think it would be better to not have my book published with them. If there is any way I can get out of the contract with them, it would be good for me. I'm almost done with the book. If you agree to edit it, it will get my foot in the door with a new publishing house. I might even be able to get more money. Of course, you will be well-compensated for your help."

I grinned. "I like the sound of that."

"I'm so glad you are getting this whole thing out in the open," she said.

"Me too."

"I'm especially glad because now I can see Vance."

"What? You still haven't called him?"

"We've exchanged a few texts, but that's it."

I groaned and shook my head. "I thought you were going to go out with him."

"I couldn't do it. I still feel like I'm carrying around this big secret. I'm terrible with secrets. I don't want to let the cat out of the bag before it's official."

"I think you are using me as an excuse not to go out with him."

She pretended to be shocked. "I would never do that!"

"Liar. What's the problem?"

"I don't know. Do you guys want to go on a double date again on Wednesday?"

I rolled my eyes. "You are acting like a seventh-grade girl. Are you afraid to be alone with him?"

"I'm not afraid of him."

"Then why are you stalling? Do you not like this guy?"

She shrugged. "I do. I think. I don't really know him."

"It's hard to get to know someone if you don't talk to them," I said dryly.

"You know why I can't talk to him."

"Piper, stop using me as an excuse. I don't care if he knows what's about to happen with Austin. I really can't imagine he'll care. It's not like we are superstars. Austin might think he is, but people don't fawn over authors like they fawn over celebrities. Real celebrities. Austin is only a celebrity in his own mind."

"True," she said with a nod. "But still. It feels like I'm gossiping."

"Yes, we'll go on your double date, and I will tell him the whole sordid story. Then you don't have to feel like you are gossiping. We'll address the elephant in the room and effectively kill it. Then there is nothing stopping you and Mr. Sexy from getting on with things. You can't use me as an excuse. And you cannot ask us to go on another double date until you've been dating for several months."

"What? Why?"

"Because you are supposed to have the honeymoon period. You need to do the new couple thing and then you can start doing the old married couple thing."

"Gee, thanks for the permission."

"I'll talk to Cooper tonight," I told her. "I'm sure he'll be on board with a dinner date."

"Good."

"All right, now I have to finish packing my room. Cooper is going to kill me if I'm not done when he gets here tonight. I've been dragging my feet."

"Uh-oh, cold feet?"

"No, not at all. Laziness. Pure laziness."

"We're close," she said with a laugh. "There's a few things in the closet. Do you want to do that or finish packing the kitchen?"

I looked at the kitchen. It was daunting. "I'll do the kitchen. I've already taken advantage of you."

"Yes, you have, which is why you are giving me a break on your editing fee."

"Oh, I am?"

"Yep. Manual labor in exchange for you kicking back and reading a great story."

"It is a pretty good story. I think you should drag your feet on this book. Don't make your deadline. Hopefully this whole thing will blow up, and you can shop your book elsewhere."

"That's the plan."

She grabbed one of the empty boxes and carried it into my bedroom. I grabbed one for myself and pulled open the kitchen drawer with all my utensils. I probably should have given most of this stuff away. Cooper had a full kitchen. Despite that, I grabbed the cutlery tray and turned it upside down.

"What the hell was that?" Piper called out from the bedroom.

"Nothing. Just packing!"

I opened the next drawer and scooped everything out and dropped it in the box. I was certain I would regret my packing habits when it came time to unpack, but that was a problem for another day. I opened another drawer and pulled out my various spatulas and what-nots.

That's when my phone rang again. "Little bastards!" I growled.

I stomped to the table and snatched the phone up. "What do you want?" I barked.

As usual, dead air. "I hope you are enjoying yourself. Learn how to breathe hard or something. You are the worst prankers ever."

The call was already disconnected by the time I looked at the screen to see it was once again a blocked number. "Fuckers."

"Prank call again?" she called out.

"Yes. The little shits need a spanking."

I heard her mumbling something, but I had no idea what she said. I was going to assume it was something about changing my number. It really was getting old. At first, the calls freaked me out. Then they just became annoying. Now it was really pissing me off. If it was Austin, which I had a feeling it was, I couldn't wait to put the screws to him. He was a coward. He couldn't even properly threaten me. So many times I wanted to call him back and scream at him. I didn't. I told myself not to give him the satisfaction of knowing he'd gotten under my skin.

I got back to work with my very expedient packing. At this rate, I was going to be done in an hour. I quickly taped up the box and labeled it before adding it to the pile. "I'm almost done!" I called out.

"Liar!"

"Nope. I'm hauling ass."

I grabbed another box and opened a cupboard to start packing my pots and pans. Piper came out of my bedroom carrying another box. "I think I'm almost done in there."

She put the box off to the side and opened the fridge. She had just opened a bottle of water when I heard what sounded like a scuffle outside my door. "What the hell?" I murmured.

My front door burst open, bouncing off the wall. Piper shrieked and dropped the bottle of water. I stared at the two very large men wearing ski masks that were now standing in the living room.

"Who are you?" I shouted. "Get out!"

Piper was standing closest to them. She reached out and grabbed the mug from my coffee earlier. She tossed it at the men and rushed toward me. "Run!" she screamed.

I looked at her wide-eyed. We were boxed in. The kitchen was a U shape. Our exit was blocked by them. There was nowhere to run. I grabbed her and shoved her behind me. Piper was a little thing. I wasn't exactly large, but I felt like I had a little more meat on my bones, which should make me stronger. In theory. We were about to find out.

"Get out. I'm calling the police!"

"Grab the blonde," one of them said.

"No!" Piper hollered. She bolted out from behind me and attacked the two men with nails out. She fought like a hellcat. She shrieked and screamed as her arms flailed. I watched for several seconds in complete shock. Then I realized what was happening. She was fighting for both our lives.

I was about to jump into the fray when one of the men swung out. His fist connected with her face. Piper dropped like a sack of potatoes on my kitchen floor. I screamed and rushed at them. I didn't know what I was going to do, but I had to fight. I had to fight with everything I had.

"No!" I screamed. "Help! Help!"

I swung my fist, hoping I could actually land a punch. I didn't know what I hit. Probably a shoulder or maybe an elbow. I felt strong arms around me, whipping me around with the other masked man in front of me. I fought like hell, kicking and scratching and trying to go limp like I had read in a self-defense thing.

"Let go of me!"

I kicked and screamed and dug deep to find more strength to fight. I felt terrible for stepping on Piper in the struggle, but there was nothing to be done about it. I sobbed as I realized my fight was futile. I was going to be killed or worse. I had never felt so week in my life.

I heard an 'oomph' followed by a curse. "Bitch! Knock her out. She just elbowed me in the balls!"

It was the last thing I heard before my world went black.

Chapter Eighteen

Cooper

I COULDN'T EAT OR SLEEP. It was nothing short of a miracle that I was able to breathe. If not for the involuntary response of my body, I was certain I would have stopped breathing as well. I rubbed my hands over my face. I wanted to wake up from the nightmare I was stuck in.

I paced my living room. It didn't make sense. Nothing made sense. "Sit down," Damon said.

"I can't."

"They'll be here soon enough," he said.

"Why is it taking so long?" I asked. I knew he couldn't tell me, but I needed answers. "Where is she?"

I had probably asked those same two questions at least a hundred times in the last twenty-four hours. No one could give me an answer. Not the cops. Not Piper. Not Damon. No one. No one could tell me a damn thing.

"They are looking for her," Damon said.

Piper came into the living room, moving a little stiffly as she sat down on the couch. She pulled the blanket over her and rested her head against one of the throw pillows from Tatum's house. "She's going to be okay," Piper said.

Her voice was hoarse. It was a combination of the screaming she'd done during the attack and all the crying she'd done since she'd come to. I couldn't stop replaying that moment over and over in my head. I couldn't stop thinking about all of the what-ifs.

"I should have been there," I said. "I should have gone straight to the apartment. I was so stupid. I was trying to turn this place into Fort Knox and the real threat was there. I left her alone. I knew there was a chance this could happen."

"You couldn't have known," Piper said. "We were just talking. Talking and teasing and then they burst through the door. I tried, Cooper. Oh my goodness, I tried so hard to help her." She started crying again.

"I know you fought like hell," I told her. "It wasn't your fault. I'm glad you weren't seriously hurt."

"Did they say anything?" Damon asked. "Like why they were there or what they wanted?"

"No. They barely said a thing. It happened fast. I managed to get in a few licks, but I didn't do any damage."

I looked at the black eye and swollen cheekbone. She had been knocked out cold when I got to the apartment. Apparently, I showed up about fifteen minutes too late. Fifteen minutes. So much could happen in fifteen minutes. I had never really understood the importance of time until last night. One minute. One second could change everything. Fifteen minutes was a lifetime.

"Where are the damn cops?" I asked with frustration. "Why can't they find her?"

"There wasn't a lot to go on," Damon said. "You need to tell them about the PI."

"What about the PI?" Piper asked.

Damon looked at me. I didn't have the energy to tell the story. I gave him a slight nod of my head and gave him permission to tell the story. I stared out the living room window as I listened to him tell her. I should have gone straight to her when I heard about the potential kidnapping.

"It was Austin!" Piper screeched. "We have to tell the police!"

"The police already know Austin had reason to be mad at her, but we can't tell them about the other stuff. We have to wait for a ransom."

"Wait?" Piper said. "We can't wait. What if they are hurting her?"

It felt like she'd physically punched me. "I can't show all my cards. If the kidnappers call, I need to be able to offer them something."

"Offer them what?" Piper said.

"The tape. The evidence the PI is digging up. I have to be ready to offer them something in exchange for her release."

"Cooper! Do you know how crazy that sounds? You're not a super-hero. You're not a detective. Tell the police."

"They are supposed to be here," I said. "They said they would come by and follow up after the interviews last night."

She fell silent. We all were quiet. The sun had set, but none of us bothered to turn on any lights. I wondered if she was in the dark. Was she afraid? That was stupid. Of course she was afraid. She would be ter-rified. Was she hoping I would save her? Was she being hurt? I had so many questions and no answers.

Headlights flashed in the driveway. I rushed for the door and pulled it open. I had some secret hope the cops had found her and were bringing her home. I prayed that's what was happening. "Do you have her?" I asked as two detectives walked toward me.

"Let's talk inside," one of them said.

They were alone. I felt like my heart was being pulled out of my chest. I stumbled back and let them in. "What do you know? Do you have any leads?"

"Why don't you have a seat, Mr. Dunn?"

Piper scooted over on the couch. I sat down next to her without completely sitting back. I was ready to jump up at any second. "What do you know?" I asked again.

"Unfortunately, forensics went through the apartment and found nothing."

"They were wearing masks and gloves," Piper said.

"Yes, but we were hoping to find something else."

"So what now?" I asked.

"We've got her picture out there and patrol is actively searching, but without any idea of what vehicle we are looking for, it's a needle in a haystack."

"So you just give up?" I asked.

"No. We will keep looking. We've reviewed surveillance cameras from the area, but so far, we haven't found anything."

Piper sobbed. "I should have fought harder."

"You mentioned there was an ex involved," the first detective said. "Tell us more about that."

"Her ex is Austin Scott. He broke up with her. Then he wanted her back. She didn't want him back."

"We did a little research and found a couple of articles and pictures."

"Don't believe that garbage," Piper spat. "It was a publicity stunt. He's got a new book coming out, and they were playing it up. Tatum did not want to be back with him."

"Was their relationship violent? Abusive?"

"No," Piper answered. "He never hurt her, but he was definitely a control freak. He is not a good guy."

"Have you talked to him?" I asked.

"We're following all the leads we have. Is there anyone else that might be involved?"

I had to keep my mouth shut. There was a lot that could still happen with the publishing company. I didn't find it even the least bit surprising she had been kidnapped the night before she was supposed to meet with the lawyers.

"There was a note left on her door," Piper blurted it out.

That got their attention. "A note? What kind of note?"

"It said we'll find you," Piper told them.

"When was this?"

"A couple weeks ago. She was also getting prank calls."

My head whipped around. "What? When?"

Piper sighed and shook her head. "It's been the last couple of days. It was just one or two and then it became an all-day thing. It was always from a blocked number. She ignored the calls, but last night, she answered one."

"And?" I asked anxiously.

"What did the caller say?" the detective asked.

"Nothing," Piper said. "Nothing at all. She was convinced it was a couple of kids making prank calls. She answered, and they never said anything. Actually, she got a call like a minute before the men broke in."

The two detectives exchanged a look. "What?" I asked. "What does that mean?"

"Do you have her phone?"

"Uh, I don't know." I looked at Piper. "Do you know where it is?"

"I don't know," she said.

"We'll check with the forensics team; they might have bagged it."

"Why do you want her phone?" I asked hopefully.

"We'll want to check her call history. We might be able to trace the call."

"Even if the number is blocked?" Piper asked.

"We can do a lot with a little," the detective answered. "Was there anything else? Any other threats?"

The three of us exchanged a look. "No," I answered. "She was moving in with me today."

"Why?" the detective asked.

I realized how bad it sounded. "We are together."

They looked at each other and then me. "This is a new thing?"

"I've known Tatum for years."

"Did the ex know you were moving in together?"

I shrugged. "I honestly don't know."

"Do you know the ex?"

"Yes. Like I said, I've known Tatum for years. I knew her before she got together with Austin."

They were giving me that same look. Like they were suddenly understanding the whole picture. "Would Austin hold a grudge against you?"

Piper made a snorting sound. "You think?"

"Have you asked Austin?" I asked them directly. "Please ask him where she is. If he has nothing to do with this, then who did? Who would come after her? Ask him."

"We're going to explore some more leads. If you hear anything, please call us right away."

I got to my feet. "And then what? What happens next? How do I find her?"

"Los Angeles is a big city. We're doing all we can."

Their words offered me no comfort. "Thanks," I muttered.

After they left, I turned to look at Damon and Piper. Piper's bruised face made me cringe. Not because she looked bad, but because if she looked like that after a minute with the kidnappers, what did Tatum look like after twenty-four hours?

"We should make flyers," Piper said.

"And create a Facebook page," Damon added. "We'll start a hashtag. The police can't look everywhere, but the internet can. We'll get everyone looking for her, at gas stations, hotels, parks, everywhere."

"What is that going to do?" I asked. "She doesn't want to be a hashtag."

"She wants to be found," Piper said. "We'll deal with her embarrassment once she's home. You heard the police. They don't know where she is. They don't know how to find her. We can't just sit here and hope she comes home. We have to find her."

I rubbed my hands over my face again. "You're right."

Damon got up. "I'll call one of those copy places and find out how much it costs to get a thousand flyers done. Piper, you start designing it."

Piper got up and grabbed the laptop she brought with her. I watched them jump into action. They were convinced a flyer was going to find her. It wasn't enough action for me. I needed to do something.

"Fuck this," I growled. I grabbed my keys and started for the door.

"Where are you going?" Piper asked.

"I'm going to hunt that motherfucker down myself."

"Wait!" Damon shouted.

"I'm going."

"You can't go to his house," Piper warned. "You're not in your right mind. If you get arrested, you will do her no good."

"I can't just sit here."

"Let's get this flyer made and we'll go make copies. We can drive around all night and hand out flyers."

"I'm going to beat the shit out of him until he tells me where she is. I know this was him. You both know it too."

"Then we should just tell the cops about the tape and the accusations. They'll look a lot harder at him. We need them to put pressure on him."

I curled my lip with disgust. "He's a snake. I bet you he's already told the cops some long sob story. He'll tell them he loves her and play the role of a worried boyfriend. I wouldn't be surprised if he told them it was me that kidnapped her."

"Let them do their jobs," Damon insisted. "We'll do what we can."

I walked out the door. I was not going to sit around. I wanted to look Austin in the eye when I asked him where the hell she was. If he tried to deny it, I would tell him I knew what he did. I would threaten his very life.

Chapter Nineteen

Tatum

I DIDN'T HAVE TO PEE, which was not a good thing. I couldn't be sure how long I had been locked in this room with windows that were boarded up. I thought it was at least a day, two days maybe. The only light in the room came from under the door. The locked door. I had tried out to get by any means necessary. I clawed at the boards over the windows. I clawed at the door hinges. My fingernails were broken and my fingertips bloody.

I had not been given any food or water since I had been snatched right out of my apartment. I still couldn't quite believe things had happened the way they did. I was kidnapped. I was actually kidnapped. I thought about the prank calls and the note on my door. There were plenty of warning signs, and I'd ignored them all.

"Stupid, Tatum, so stupid."

I lay on the floor. I was too weak to do much of anything else. I was worried about Piper. I had no idea if she was alive or in another room. I prayed they'd left her alone. It was clear the men had been there for me. She was hurt because she was with me. That killed me to think she'd been seriously hurt because of something I did.

My thoughts drifted to Cooper. That's where my thoughts tended to be most of the time. He had to know I was gone by now. I wondered what he was doing. Was he looking for me? Yes, he was. He would be searching the city for me. I hated that he was suffering. I knew he was going to be worried out of his mind. This was so unfair to him.

I couldn't feel sorry for him. Not right now. I needed to focus on getting out of here, wherever here was. Cooper would find me. He would rescue me. He was my hero. I just had to hold on a little longer. "I'll wait for you."

I closed my eyes. I wasn't sure how much I had slept since I had been kidnapped, but it felt like a lot. I drifted in and out of consciousness. Or delirium. I had no idea which. I knew my head hurt like hell. It could have been from lack of food and water or it could have been from the big brutes knocking my ass out. I had no idea what they had done to me while I had been knocked out. My body ached all over. Again, I wasn't sure if they'd dropped my ass or beat the shit out of me.

I woke up to bright light pouring into the room. At first, I was confused. My brain struggled to make sense of what I was seeing. "Hello?" I murmured. My voice was harsh. I could feel my lips sticking together and my tongue felt thick.

"Turn on the light," someone said.

I pushed myself up and blinked several times. I recognized the voice, but I wanted to see his face. "Austin, what are you doing? Why are you doing this?"

"Bring in those pillows," he said instead of answering my question.

"What's going on?" I asked.

Three throw pillows were tossed at me. It seemed a little ridiculous to give me pillows now. Comfort was the least of my concern. I heard heels coming toward the door of the room I was in.

"She's awake?" Wendy asked as she walked into the room.

My mouth fell open. I couldn't believe what I was seeing. "Wendy?"

More footsteps. It was a regular fucking party. "No fucking way," I muttered when Mr. Simms walked into the room.

"This is all on you," Austin said with disgust.

"What is on me?"

"This whole mess," he snapped. "Look what you made us do."

It was the most ludicrous thing I had ever heard. "Look what I made you do?" I said on a hoarse laugh. "You kidnapped me. You've imprisoned me. How in the world did I make you do that?"

"All you had to do was stay with me. You could have been my girlfriend again and we could have been rich. I was prepared to marry you one day. You would have been the wife of a successful, wealthy author. I have an offer for a movie deal."

"Too bad none of that is real. You didn't write the book!"

"You should have minded your own business," Wendy said. "You couldn't just let it go. None of this is your concern. You meddled in something that did not have anything to do with you. Why? Why would you do that?"

"Because what you are doing is wrong?"

Gary stepped forward. "My company is not doing anything illegal. Your little crusade is not going to get anyone anything. Everyone has been happy with the arrangements. You didn't have to go digging."

"I didn't dig! It fell in my lap. Austin, you know this is wrong. Why can't you just write your own stuff?"

"I do write," Austin scoffed.

I rolled my eyes. "You write a word here and there. You don't write stories." I turned to look at Wendy and Gary. "Shame on the two of you for promoting this behavior. It's theft. Plain and simple. You are stealing the hard work of real authors. You are stealing money out of their pockets."

"They are generously paid for their work," Gary said. He didn't look the least bit bothered by the situation. He looked cool as a cucumber, like he regularly kidnapped people.

"They are not generously paid for a damn thing! You give them pennies compared to what you pay Austin."

"I think Wendy said it already. It's none of your business."

"I made it my business."

"And look where that got you," he said with a laugh. "You act like you're Nancy Drew. Do you really think you can outsmart me? You don't think I've covered my ass?"

He sounded evil. The friendly, congenial man I thought I knew was gone. I couldn't believe he was acting so vicious. "I don't know why you're mad at me," I said. "I was trying to help you and the company. You know plagiarizing is wrong. You know what you are doing is wrong. You can't steal their work and slap his name on it."

"We can," Wendy said with a laugh. "We will. You can't stop this. You are talking about a multi-million-dollar practice. We are doing this for the people. This is a victimless offense."

"It's a crime," I corrected her. "And there are victims. If you like the books, why not buy them from the original authors and pay them what you pay him?"

"That is not your concern," Gary said. "If I were you, I'd be more concerned with your role in all of this."

"I've done nothing!"

"You'll have to pay for your crime," Wendy said.

It was like I was in the Twilight Zone. "What are you talking about? I've committed no crime."

"Against me," Austin seethed. "I'm the man you love, and you were going to have me thrown in jail. What kind of woman does that?"

"I don't love you. I'm the kind of woman who cannot stand by and watch people destroy others."

"No one was destroyed," Wendy said with a laugh. "You're so dramatic. Maybe you are hoping to be a writer one day."

"And have you steal my work? No thank you. Where am I?"

I didn't expect an answer, but it seemed like I had to ask. I felt like I should be fighting or trying to make an escape. Unfortunately, I had so little energy. Even the verbal sparring with them was taking a toll.

"You're in LA," Austin answered and earned a glare from the other two. I got the feeling they were not happy with him.

"It doesn't matter where you are," Wendy said. "You could be in LA or New York. No one is going to find you, and you won't be escaping."

"Just let me go. You've proven your point. You wanted to scare me. You don't want me to tell anyone about your disgusting, immoral practices. I get it. Let me go."

"Can't do that," Gary said. "You've caused some problems for us. You and that PI."

My head popped up. "What?"

"Oh, you didn't think I didn't know about that, did you?" He smirked. "I know everything. Your little PI violated about twenty laws when he broke into our intranet. He's not coming to find you because he's on his way to jail."

"No," I breathed. "You're lying."

"Am I? Do you really think I'm dumb enough to leave myself exposed to just any old Joe Schmo off the street? There are plans in place for things like this. Contingencies that will ensure my company remains at the top, right where it belongs."

I couldn't believe what I was hearing. It was so, so wrong. Despair threatened to pull me into the black hole it had been trying to drag me into since they attacked me. "What about Piper?" I asked Austin. "Did they kill her?"

"No. She's fine."

At least he had enough of a conscience to give me that much. "I want to go home. I won't tell anyone about this or the stolen property."

"It isn't stolen if I bought and paid for it," Wendy snapped.

I looked at the woman who'd been my boss for two years. It was like looking at a stranger. The woman in front of me was on the border of being unhinged. She was angry and had a very wild look in her eyes. "Please, let me go. I won't say anything."

"Too late," Austin said, and I was almost convinced I heard a little sadness in his voice. "You've done it now."

"How long do you plan on keeping me in here?" I asked.

"You're not the only target," Wendy said with a laugh. "You're the bait. We prefer to handle these things with one fell swoop. It's much tidier when it can be handled as one job versus several."

I didn't want to believe what I was hearing. "Cooper?" I whispered.

"Cooper and that stupid PI," Austin growled. "They're on my ass. He sent the cops after me already."

"You're kind of the obvious suspect," I reminded him.

"Don't get cocky," he snapped. "Look around you. You don't get to be cocky. I win. You lose."

"How long?" I asked.

"Until it's done," Wendy answered with zero inflection in her voice.

I looked back at Austin. He was the weakest link. If there was any chance I was going to get out of this, he was going to be the one to break. I hoped. "I need to use the bathroom," I said in a small voice. "Please."

"The other room is ready," Wendy said. "Take her in there."

"Other room?" I asked.

"Get up," Austin barked.

Gary pulled a gun from inside his suit jacket. "Run and I shoot. Trust me, I'm an excellent aim."

I almost vomited when I saw the gun. My first thought was how many times had I seen and talked to Gary when he'd been armed? I struggled to get up. Austin grabbed my arm and jerked me up before pushing me in front of him. Wendy led the way down a dark hall covered with the ugliest wallpaper I had ever seen. The building was old. I was guessing fifties or sixties. There were several doors with numbers faded into the ugly brown paint on each door. It was an apartment building or possibly a hotel.

Wendy opened a door. Once again, the windows had all been boarded up. There was a cot in the corner and a single chair. The rest of the room was empty. The remnants of where a kitchen would have once been was in one corner. "Bathroom is through that door," Wendy said.

"Now what?" I asked them. "What are you going to do with me now?"

"You'll wait patiently like a good little girl," Wendy cackled.

The three of them left, slamming the door behind them. I heard the lock, but I had to try. Once again, I was locked in a prison. I walked to where the windows had been and tried to pry off the boards. There wasn't a chance in hell that was going to happen. I didn't even know how high up we were. If I did manage to get a window open, was I really going to jump from the tenth floor or however high up we were?

I went into the bathroom and nearly vomited at the smell. I had to leave the door open to take advantage of the light coming in from the main room. There was a single toilet and a sink. The tub had been torn out.

As I was exploring my prison and looking for something that could be used for a weapon, I heard footsteps. The door opened again. Austin smiled at me. It was just a little creepy. He reached out and flipped on a light switch. "We're not cave people," he said with a laugh. "Have a little light."

I couldn't believe I had gone to the bathroom in the dark when all I had to do was try the switch. "Let me out of here, Austin. You're not this guy. You aren't a felon. What you guys are doing is a felony. You'll go to prison. Just let me go, and we'll pretend this didn't happen."

"No, we won't," he said and thrust a bag at me. "Eat. I loathe skinny women."

"What?"

"It's a burger and fries. Here's a bottle of water to wash it down."

"You're feeding me?"

"Like Wendy said, you're the bait. We can't have you dead. We need you alive to bring them in."

"Austin! Stop this!" I stomped my foot.

"Eat your dinner, Tatum. You never know when it might be your last."

He walked out of the room and locked the door once again. Now that I could see my prison, I was even more repulsed. Evidence of mice and roaches was everywhere. It was a horrible, disgusting place, and I didn't have a way out. The bag in my hand smelled amazing. It could be poisoned, I told myself. I was willing to take my chances.

Chapter Twenty

Cooper

I DROVE DOWN THE STREET with my head on a swivel. I wasn't sure what I was expecting to see. If she was walking down the street, she would have already called me. I wasn't going to find her coming out of a store or sitting on a park bench. It was the most helpless feeling in the world. I couldn't do a damn thing to help her.

I pulled into the coffee shop where I was meeting Alan the PI. My brain was fried. I knew I looked like a shitshow. My eyes were bloodshot. I hadn't showered since yesterday, and I probably stank. Alan was sitting a table with his laptop open.

"Anything?" I asked and sat down.

He looked at me and visibly cringed. He pushed a cup toward me. "Drink that."

I had been running on coffee and Red Bull for days. I wasn't sure how much more my body could take before I collapsed. "Thanks. Do you have anything new?"

He slowly shook his head. "The guy went off the grid."

"What about the guy that was following him that day? What exactly did he say?"

"Cooper, we've been over this. He followed him to the dry cleaners. Austin went in and never came out. My guy couldn't have known he was going to ditch him."

"I can't do this," I told him. "I can't."

"I'm digging into this. I'm tracking his credit cards."

"And? Anything?"

He shook his head again. "No. He's gone underground. He has to know the cops are on to him."

"Why aren't the cops looking for him?"

"They are," he assured me.

"They won't return my calls. They won't tell me anything. It's been three days, Alan. Three fucking days! She could be anywhere!"

"It's unlikely they got her out of the city. I'm digging into their backgrounds. I'm going to find her."

I wanted to believe him. It was all I had to hang on to. "Fine. I'm going to pick up Damon. He wants to put up another thousand flyers."

"You're doing the right thing," he told me. "Get her face out there. Someone saw something."

"I'm offering a reward," I told him.

He hissed. "That's not a good idea. You're going to get all kinds of bullshit tips that waste time."

"I have to do something."

"Give me some time. I'm working on it."

"Three fucking days," I barked. "Three days. How much time do you need? She is suffering!"

I walked out of the coffee shop and got back in my truck. Damon was doing all he could to help, but nothing felt like it was enough. I drove to his house and slammed my hand on the horn. He came out, carrying a box.

He opened the door and pushed the box into the center. "I got another thousand for free. The guy at the copy shop got his boss to write it off."

"Thanks."

"How are you doing?" he asked.

"Fine."

"Did you get any sleep last night?"

"Not really."

I hit the gas and started down the street. "Did you go out looking again last night?"

"Yes."

"You have to get some sleep," he told me. "You are going to go down and go down hard."

"I can't stop looking. I can't just give up. How am I supposed to crawl into my warm bed and sleep when I don't know where she is? She could be lying in a ditch. She could be locked up in a cage with no food or water."

"Look, I get it. I know you're worried. We all are, but if you are going to help, you have to take care of yourself. Go by McDonald's."

"I'm not going to fucking McDonald's."

"I'm hungry, and you need to eat."

"I'm not hungry!" I shouted. "Everyone needs to stop telling me to eat. I don't want to eat. I want to find her. Why is that so damn hard for people to understand?"

"We understand you are worried. We all want to find her, but when we do find her, she's going to need you to be strong. She's going to be traumatized. You have to be strong for her. You have to be her rock. If you are in a bad way, you can't be there for her. Don't you think that should be your priority?"

I shot him a dirty look. "I'm going to the south to put up more flyers. Did you bring that staple gun?"

"We need another one."

I growled with frustration. "All I needed was a fucking staple gun."

"And you have it, but we used the shit out of it yesterday. They're cheap. We need another one."

I didn't mean to be such a dick to him, but damn if I could rein in my anger. I was angry with myself and Austin. I was angry with everyone. I saw a hardware store and pulled in. We bought two staple guns, but before he would get back in the truck, he insisted we get sandwiches from the small shop next door.

He wasn't going to give it up. I ate half my sandwich to appease him, but I did it while driving to a side of town I never really ventured into. I didn't want to admit it, but I did feel better. I had renewed strength and was ready to hit the pavement to pass out more flyers.

"I swear, when I find Austin, I'm going to kill him," I muttered as we walked down the street.

"Let the police handle it. You can't get your hands dirty with this one."

"The police aren't doing shit. They can't even find him."

"They will. They have a lot more resources than you do. It might not seem like they are doing anything, but you have to know they are still looking."

"Do I? We live in a massive city. I'm sure there are kidnappings and murders every day. Several a day. They have their hands full. Tatum is nothing to them. It's going to be up to us to find her. We are the ones that care about her. We are the ones looking in every corner."

"And we won't stop looking until we find her."

"Damn straight. Austin is going to come up for air. He can't hide forever. When he does, I'm going to beat the shit out of him. I know he's got a hand in this. The fucker is so worried about losing his money that I know he would do anything to stop her from revealing who he really is. The cops should have arrested him that night. They should have listened to me! Now he's gone. They gave him time to get away."

"Like you said, he's going to reappear. When he does, the cops are going to get him. His absence makes him look guilty. They are going to be looking at him very hard."

"They need to do a lot more than look at him. They need to drag his ass to jail."

"They will," he said again. "In the meantime, we need to do our part. We keep looking and talking to people."

"We need to get flyers with his picture on it," I said and stopped walking. "We find Austin, we find her. He's not imprisoned. He's a public figure. Someone will recognize him."

"I don't know if we can do that," he said hesitantly.

"Why the fuck not? If he can kidnap her, I can sure as hell look for his ass."

"Because you are assuming he did it. You don't have proof. Like you said, he's a public figure. If you go out there blasting his name and accusing him of kidnapping, you are putting yourself in a bad position. You have to keep a level head. You have to keep your temper under control. You are not going to do her any good if you lose your shit."

I took a deep breath. The guy was riding my last nerve. "I'm done," I said and posted one last flyer. "I'm going back to her place and then my house."

"I'll stay out here and catch a cab back home."

"She's coming home," I told him.

"I know."

I didn't think he was quite as positive as he was trying to be. "You want me to do this flyer nonsense because you're trying to keep me busy. You don't think she's coming back."

"I do think she's coming back."

"Why are we out here doing this? You know it's futile."

"Because you're right, I am trying to keep you busy. I'm trying to keep you busy so you don't go after him. I have no doubt in my mind Tatum will be back any minute. She is going to want you there for her. She is going to need you. If you do anything to Austin, you're going to jail. There won't be any hiding it was you. Do you really think that's the best thing for her? You guys just got together. You can't walk away from her now."

"I'm not walking away."

"You'll be dragged away. You'll be locked up. What if you don't get Austin? Then he's free to keep doing what he's doing, and you're the one paying for a crime. She'll be on the outside with him."

The very thought curled my stomach. The sandwich he'd practically forced me to eat was threatening to come back up. "I won't get caught."

I walked away, my long legs eating up the sidewalk as I made my way back to my truck. Her face haunted me as I passed telephone poles with her flyer stapled to them. Her eyes haunted me. I could not imagine my life without her in it. Not getting her back wasn't an option. I would kill Austin if anything happened to her. I would gladly spend the rest of my days in prison if it meant I got to rid the world of that vile piece of scum.

I did what I always did. I drove back to the places I knew Tatum was most familiar with. I knew I wasn't going to see her in the coffee shop she always went to, but I went anyway. I wanted to believe this was all a big misunderstanding and she was just out of town for a few days.

When I walked in, I saw Piper. She was sitting at a table and staring blankly at the wall. Her friend was torn up as well. The bruising on her face was fading a little. It was just another reminder of how long Tatum had been gone.

"Hi," I said and sat down at the table.

Piper looked at me. There were unshed tears in her eyes. "She's not here."

I grabbed her hand and squeezed. "I know."

"I woke up this morning and for a split second, I forgot. I forgot what happened. Then I convinced myself that maybe it was a nightmare. You know the kind that feel very real but once you get on with your day, you can shake the feeling. I came here and hoped I would run into her with a cup of coffee in hand as she rushed out the door to get to work. She's not here."

"We'll find her."

She blinked back the tears. "I should have fought harder."

I knew the guilt she was carrying because I felt the same way. I had raked myself over the coals. I couldn't stop thinking of all the different ways I could have prevented the tragedy if I had done this or that. If I had told her there was a kidnapping plot. If I had gotten her that pepper spray I'd thought about. If I had gone straight to her place instead of Home Depot.

"You did everything you could," I assured her. "You fought two big guys. That takes balls. This isn't on you."

She wiped the tears. "We should have locked the door."

"They would have kicked it in. They were determined to get her. No one could stop them."

"She has to be okay."

"She will be. Did you walk here?"

She nodded. "I really, really wanted to believe this was just another day. I wanted to believe I would see her. We'd talk about my book and everything would be normal."

"Let me drive you home," I told her. "You shouldn't be out here alone."

"Let him come for me," she hissed. "This time I'll be ready for him. I will kick his ass."

I had to fight back a smile. "I have no doubt in my mind you will do just that, but if he brings backup, you could be in trouble."

I convinced her to let me take her home. She was going to make more phone calls and do everything she could to get Tatum's face on the news. I appreciated all her effort. I knew it made her feel better to be doing something. For me, it wasn't enough. I had to be physically looking. I had a nervous energy inside of me that wouldn't be quieted. I felt like I was still riding an adrenaline high. It wouldn't let me out of its grip. I was going to drop like a ton of bricks eventually, but not yet. Not until I knew she was safe.

Chapter Twenty-One

Tatum

SCARED WOULD BE AN understatement to describe how I felt. I really thought they would hold me for a day or two and then let me go once they were certain I wasn't going to talk. When I woke up hours after I had eaten the burger and fries, I realized I was still stuck. They were taking this hostage thing seriously. I wasn't going to be released to go back to my life.

"Food," I heard a male say when the door opened. A plastic bag was tossed into the room before the door slammed shut once again.

I didn't recognize the voice. It wasn't Austin or Gary, which meant there were more people involved with my kidnapping. I opened the bag and found a deli sandwich with a pack of chips and two more bottles of water.

I supposed the fact they were feeding me was a good thing. They were keeping me alive. For how long I didn't know, but I would take every minute I could get. That brought me one minute closer to Cooper rescuing me. I knew it was a pipe dream. This was the real world. Cooper wasn't some superhero. If I was rescued, it would be police storming the door. And that was one very big if.

I ate my sandwich while standing. The floor was disgusting. The cot was decent, but I so wanted a shower. The running water in the place was more like running rust. It was gross, and I wasn't about to use it to try and clean up. I had no idea if it was day or night outside. I didn't know how long I had been captive. I knew nothing. The world could be gone for all I knew.

When I heard footsteps outside the door, I braced myself for whatever was coming my way. This could be the moment. I could be getting rescued or killed. Wendy walked through the door wearing one of her usual perfectly tailored business suits. She looked very out of place in the squalid condition of the apartment.

"Oh goodness, Tatum," she said and waved a hand in front of her nose. "How do you stand it in here? It reeks."

I was assuming that was a rhetorical question. "Are you letting me go?"

"No. Not yet. Maybe not ever."

"Great. I understand I'm your prisoner, but don't feel like you need to visit. I'd prefer it if you didn't."

"Always so snarky," she said with a laugh.

"Captivity makes me cranky."

"You could have avoided all of this if you had just left things alone. I told you to leave it be. You are a self-righteous goody two shoes who thinks your shit doesn't stink. You thought you were so cool when you were dating Austin. You walked around the office like you were the queen. I always wondered what he saw in you. You are not all that pretty, and you could stand to lay off the cake and brownies a bit."

"You like Austin?" I said with surprise.

She scoffed. "Austin is too young and too dumb for me. I prefer my men to have a little more between the ears than a lot of fluff. Austin is attractive enough, and I didn't mind sleeping with him on occasion, but I could never date him."

I wasn't going to react. She was trying to goad me. She wanted me to be jealous. I could care less if she slept with Austin. That didn't exactly make her special. Austin wasn't all that selective with who he slept with, I had learned.

"What do you want, Wendy?"

"I was on my way into the office and thought I would stop by and see how far you had fallen. I probably shouldn't tell you this, but it makes me very happy to see you like this."

"Why? Why do you hate me? I thought we were friends."

She waved a hand. "You're an editor. You aren't my friend. I played nice, but you've always gotten on my nerves."

"Is that why I'm a prisoner? Because I annoyed you?"

"That and other reasons. Just be glad Austin convinced me to let you be in this room. I would have loved to leave you in the other apartment without a toilet. You deserve to be taken down a peg or ten."

"What have I ever done to you to make me hate me?"

"You always act like you are so much better than everyone else. You walk around with your head held high and pretend to like everyone, but I know better. You're one of those judgmental bitches that thinks she's the ultimate gift to the world. You thought that dating Austin made you someone special. When he dumped you, I couldn't have been happier. Finally, he dumped the dead weight. We'd been on him for months to do it. We were only grateful he heeded our advice and left you at home when he had to make public appearances."

"What are you talking about? I've never stuck my nose in the air at you or anyone else."

"Oh please. You walked into that job interview that first day with your tits hanging out and that wide-eyed innocent expression. You did that to impress Gary. I never would have hired you, but he was taken with you. He was only interested in your tits and boy, did you make sure he noticed them. Always wearing those low-cut blouses and purposely making your nipples hard to get him to notice you."

I was revolted at the very thought. "I did no such thing. Not even close."

"It's fine," she said as if I had never said a word. "I know your kind. Your kind is what pushed me out of the career I loved and into one I find boring. I was no longer the prettiest girl in the room. I was stuck behind a desk making stars out of all the people Gary brought through the door. He loves a pretty face. He doesn't care if it's male or female. If he sees something he likes, he snatches it up and makes them a star."

"I take it he didn't do that with you."

I couldn't help but get in a few barbs. I was offended that she thought I'd used my boobs to get a job.

"Oh, Gary saw something special in me. He knew I could polish a turd, so to speak."

"What are you talking about? Are you drunk?"

"Don't be a smartass. I'm not drunk."

I had no idea what she was talking about. I had a feeling the woman was suffering some kind of mental illness. I hadn't noticed it before, but maybe she knew how to hide it well. She wasn't hiding anything now. Her crazy was on full display.

"Fine, what do you want? I don't know what you want me to say. I never flashed my boobs at Gary. I got that job because I'm good at what I do."

"I was good at what I did."

"Which was?"

"I could have been the next Danielle Steele or Nora Roberts. I was good at what I did. I wrote books that sophisticated women enjoyed. I was better than these hacks that come through our doors."

"That I am going to agree with you on," I told her. "The hacks are exactly that. They are talentless authors that have pretty faces."

"I had a pretty face!" She stomped her foot. "I could have been one of the best authors that company has. Gary didn't see it. He wanted me to be the manager of the talent. He refused to read my manuscripts. He said I was too old, and no one was interested in old authors. He wanted young and cutting edge. He put me on the shelf before I got to have my time in the sun!"

Yep, she was definitely riding the cuckoo train. "It sounds like you have an issue with Gary. Maybe you should lock him in here."

"You're not funny."

"I'm not trying to be. I just don't understand why you hate me. I've done nothing to you, Wendy. I thought we were friends. You are the one who encouraged me to go after Cooper. You never let on that you hated me."

She smiled. It was all teeth and very creepy. "That's because I'm an actress."

I blinked and tried to remember when that had been brought up. "You're a what?"

She made a big show of being put out to answer questions from a peasant. "I was an actress. A child actress. I could have been the next big thing, but one day, I developed breasts. I couldn't get the kid parts anymore and I was told I didn't have the looks to be a leading lady. One day I was a child star and the next no one knew my name. I tried to evolve. I tried to change my appearance. I even got these!" She lifted her breasts that I had long suspected were cosmetically enhanced, but now I knew for sure.

"I'm sorry that happened to you," I said in an attempt to appease her. She was going off the rails. I wasn't sure what she would do when that happened.

"No you're not! No one is. People like you that are blessed with natural beauty don't understand what it's like. I stopped acting and started writing. My stuff was good. I could have been a screenwriter if someone would have given me a chance. No one would give me a chance!"

I nodded as if I understood. I didn't. I had no idea how I was involved in any of this. But I was going to keep her talking. The door was open. If I could distract her, I might be able to escape. "It's a tough business to get into."

"Not for you!" she shouted. "You walked in with your blond hair and big tits and you got the job almost immediately. I had to fight and claw my way to the top. It isn't fair."

"I went to school on a scholarship and I worked very hard to get my degree. Your place was not the first place I applied. I had to fight to get that job."

"No, you didn't. It was handed to you, just like everything else in this world. You had Austin on your arm, and you didn't treat him like the king he is. He could have been great for you."

"Austin was not a good boyfriend and he cheated on me constantly. You just admitted you were one of the women who slept with him."

"Big deal. He was still going home to you every night."

"No, no he wasn't. Our relationship fizzled out the last two years we were together. It happened right around the time he got that first book deal. Maybe the guilt made it difficult to look me in the eyes. Tell me something, Wendy, did you encourage him to steal or did he do that on his own?"

"Oh please, get off your high horse. You act like we committed a crime. Everyone got paid. Everyone was fine until you had to go butting your nose in. You just couldn't leave it alone. How selfish are you? You can't let other people have a little happiness."

"I wasn't trying to take away your happiness. My concern was for the authors that were getting screwed over. You'll still make the same money if you pay them for the books instead of posers like Austin."

"You don't get it!" she shouted. "Austin is a pawn. He's the guy we put on the back of the cover because he's attractive. He doesn't make what a real author makes. Gary does! I do. You think you're so smart and you had it all figured out, but you didn't. You're just as stupid as your boyfriend."

She lunged at me, and before I could defend myself, she slapped me across the face before shoving me hard. I stumbled backwards and fell on my ass. Wendy was charging at me like a raging bull. She slapped once and then backhanded me as she reared her arm back ready to hit me again.

A man stepped behind her and casually put an arm around her waist and dragged her back. "You stupid bitch!" she screamed at me. "You think you're so smart! I can run circles around you!"

The man never said a word as he removed her from the apartment and locked the door behind him. I couldn't move from the floor. My face burned. The backhand with her many rings had cut my cheek. I could feel blood trickling down my face, but I didn't wipe it. I couldn't do anything but stare at the door. I had no idea if she was coming back. I was shaken to my core. She always seemed so normal. I would have never guessed she was a fucking lunatic.

I slowly got back to my feet. I found a napkin in the bag that held my sandwich and dabbed at the blood on my face. The gravity of my situation slowly sank in. I was in deep shit. I had been in the mindset this wasn't real. I kept thinking it was all just for show and they were going to let me go anytime. I just had to hold on a little longer.

Now, I wasn't so sure about that. The look in Wendy's eyes terrified me. She hated me. She truly hated me, and I had no doubt in my mind she wanted me dead. "Oh shit," I whispered. I was going to die.

Chapter Twenty-Two

Cooper

I DROVE TO THE GYM like a bat out of hell. I was supposed to look normal. That was a tall order I wasn't even going to try and achieve. I parked my truck and walked into the gym. I was supposed to be meeting Alan. He'd sent me a cryptic message last night letting me know they were on to him. I didn't care if they knew we were coming for them.

Alan was in a pair of sweats and a hoodie. He looked like an average dude at the gym. I gave him a slight jerk of the head to tell him to go into the office. I went first, waiting for him to show up. He walked in and closed the door behind him.

"Were you followed?" he asked.

"I don't think so. Were you?"

"If I was, they will hopefully buy the gym act."

"Why are they following you?"

"I'm digging into their business. They aren't happy about it."

I looked at him and realized what he was saying. "Are you in danger?"

He smirked. "Always."

"I'm sorry," I told him. "I didn't mean to drag you into this mess. I had no idea it was this twisted."

"Load this," he said and handed me a thumb drive.

"What is it?" I asked and pulled out my laptop that I kept in the office.

"It's the information I found along with a mountain of evidence. There is enough here to bury them for the rest of their lives. They are finished."

"But what about Tatum?" I didn't give a shit about the theft. I wanted Tatum.

He took my laptop from me and punched a few keys and then turned it back to me. "This is what you want to see."

I stared at a Google maps screenshot. There was a red dot on a building. "What am I looking at?"

He clicked the arrow button. An image of what I assumed was the building in the first screenshot. "This apartment building."

"Okay," I said. "And? It looks like a condemned building."

"It looks that way, but there is a single residence in that building."

I was losing patience. "Are you telling me that is where Tatum is?"

"I'm telling you the head honcho at that publishing company owns that building. Wendy Kirpatrick owns it. She bought it almost thirty years ago through a trust. Apparently she was a child actor and had a lot of money. Had is the key word."

"Is Tatum there?" I asked again. I really didn't give a shit about Wendy's money or lack of.

"I don't know, but the only residence associated with that address is tied to a dummy company. I found that to be a little strange. I have an IT guy who could really dig deep into the dark web. What I found sent chills down my spine."

I looked at him. "What did you find?"

"That address was used to wire money to known hitmen."

I felt my knees go weak. I sat before I fell. My head was swimming with a million thoughts. "Hitmen?" I rasped the word. "She's dead?"

"No, no. I don't know that. I'm saying this address is mired in a number of crimes. We know Wendy owns the building. Connect the dots, and we know she is knee-deep in this nonsense."

"Did she order a hit on Tatum? Is that what happened? Am I ever going to find her?"

"I'm not giving up hope. We've connected at least two missing persons to Wendy, and right now we are operating under the assumption she ordered their hits."

"Why?"

"They were authors of books the publishing house has published under another author's name. This is something they've been doing for a while."

"Holy shit," I breathed. I couldn't believe what I was hearing. It was incomprehensible. "How did she get mixed up in this?"

"I'm not sure. We are on this. I've got a friend on the force. He is taking this very seriously. I'm handing over whatever I find to him. He's doing whatever he has to do to get it into the right hands."

"But what about Tatum?"

"I'm working on it."

I stared at the screen. "I'm going there." I grabbed a pen and wrote down the address.

"Just hold on," he warned. "You can't go storming in there. We need to operate under the assumption these people are armed. We don't know how big this network is."

"I'm not going to sit here. If there is a chance she is in that building, I'm not going to sit here."

"I understand. I had a feeling you would say that. I'm ready to help you, but we needed to plan and strategize." He handed me a scrap of paper. "Meet me here in twenty minutes. Make sure you are not followed. You leave now and I'll leave soon."

I wasn't familiar with the game of cloak and dagger. I was out of my depth. I walked to my truck and tried to look casual. I didn't see anyone watching. Then again, if they were good, I wouldn't see them. I drove to the address and realized it was in the vicinity of the apartment building I wanted to go to.

Alan showed up a few minutes later. "What are we doing here?" I asked.

"Let's go in," he said.

The house was old, small, and looked like it would crumble any day. I followed him in. There was old furniture, and the place smelled musty. "What is this place?"

He smirked. "It's my hideout. Your little friend has decided I shouldn't be alive. I'm hiding in plain sight right under her nose. They never think to look in their own backyard."

"What do you mean she doesn't think you should be alive?"

"My IT guy called and let me know I have been added to her hitlist."

"Her actual hitlist?"

"Yep, so it'd be really great if we could find this lady and get her locked up before she has me pushing up daisies."

"Holy shit. I'm so sorry."

"Don't be. I knew the risks when I took the job. We haven't found it yet, but you'll want to watch your back. She's probably got a hit on you as well."

"I'll keep that in mind. So what are we doing here?"

"We are going to watch and wait. We need to see who comes and goes from that building."

"No," I said and shook my head. "I'm not going to sit and wait. I want to go in."

"That's stupid and a death sentence. You're no good to her dead."

"How long?"

"How long what?"

"How long am I supposed to just sit here?"

"As long as it takes. There is cold beer and water in the ice chest in the kitchen. Settle in and let's see what they've got going on. I don't expect they are going to be too cautious. They don't think anyone knows about this place. That works to our advantage."

"I need to let Piper and Damon know. They check on me every hour."

He was already sitting in front of the window with the curtains drawn. There was a camera angled out of the curtains and connected to a large screen that allowed us to peep without fear of being seen. I walked away and called Damon first to let him know I was alive and well and not doing anything stupid.

"I'm watching a building that she might be in," I told Piper when she answered her phone.

"You're doing what?"

"Alan found a building that we think she could be in. We don't know. We are doing some surveillance. I'll let you know if anything happens."

"Cooper! What are you saying?" She was shrieking. I should have known she wouldn't take it quite as well as Damon had. "Go get her!"

"I don't know if she's in there. If I go in half-cocked, it does no one any good."

"But what if she is in there?"

"Piper, trust me, I want her back too. It's killing me to wait, but I can't just storm an apartment building. I have to know what I'm dealing with and if she's even in there."

"Please call me the second you know anything."

"I will. Piper, if you can go somewhere safe, you should."

"What do you mean? I'm at home."

"We've uncovered some stuff, and I don't think you're safe. I'll have Damon go sit with you. Keep your doors locked."

"You're scaring me," she said.

"I know. I'm sorry, but we can't have you getting snatched next."

Chapter Twenty-Three

Tatum

I WAS LOSING HOPE. I told myself I couldn't give up, but I was. I was resigned to my fate. They were going to kill me. I wasn't necessarily afraid of dying. I hoped they made it a fast death. I was assuming they would shoot me. Wasn't that how people killed people? I didn't know. I was out of my depth.

The part that bothered me was the fact I wouldn't get to see Cooper again. I wasn't going to get the chance to tell him how much I loved him. I knew he knew I loved him, but I wanted it to be the last thing I said to him. I wanted it to be the last thing in my heart and mind when I left this world.

A sob escaped my throat as I tumbled down a rabbit hole. I wasn't going to get the chance to be married. I would never hold my own child in my arms. I would never get to see Cooper grow old. I looked back on my twenty-six years and realized I'd wasted a lot of time. I should have dumped Austin years ago. I could have spent the last few years with Cooper being happy and truly loved.

"Oh Piper," I whispered as my thoughts turned to her. She was going to carry guilt for my death. I knew her well, and she was going to think this was her fault. I hated that I couldn't tell her it was fine. That she had done everything she could.

My pity party was taking hold when the door was flung open. My first thought was this was the moment I died. I sat up on the cot and looked at Austin. He leaned against the wall and folded his arms over his chest.

"You have made a real mess," he said.

"Me? I didn't steal books and slap my name on them and get paid thousands of dollars."

"I came in here because we need to talk. I'm hoping you can be reasonable, and we can come to some kind of agreement."

I almost jumped at the chance. I was very anxious to do just about anything if it meant I got to walk out that place. "What?"

"So the way I see it, we have a few options. We can release you, but that proves problematic for us because we can't trust you. However, we don't necessarily want your blood on our hands. That causes more problems."

It was ridiculous to hear him talk about my death and how it was a problem for him. "I won't tell anyone," I said. We both knew I was lying. I was going to sing like a bird the moment I was free.

"Yeah right. Killing you makes the most sense. It eliminates the problem. Unfortunately, Wendy thinks it could also lead to more problems. That stupid PI you hired has too much information. There are too many fingers pointed our way if you don't go home."

"You don't have to kill me."

"I have another solution," he said. I realized he already knew the solution the whole time. He was just enjoying screwing with me.

"What would that be?"

"You will be allowed to live and go about your life, but you will be my ghostwriter. You will exclusively write for me. I won't have to worry about this little problem ever creeping up again. You'll owe your life to me."

"I'm not a writer. I'm an editor."

"You can do both."

I shook my head. "There is no way I could produce the kind of books you've been stealing. Your fan base would know. It won't work."

He sighed and pulled a gun from behind him. "I was afraid you would say that. In fact, it's exactly what Gary said. I was only trying to help you out. You don't have a job. I'd be willing to pay you a small portion of the money I earn from the sales of the books you write. You get to live and get paid. I think that's a win-win situation, but alas, you want to do it the hard way."

He waved the gun around. Fear gripped me. "Fine, I'll do it. I'll write for you."

He smiled. "I thought you might change your mind."

I nodded, swallowing the fear. "I'll do it. I'll be your ghost writer. I'll figure out how to get better at writing."

He sauntered toward me. He lifted the gun over his head while he stood over me. He leaned down and tried to kiss me. I couldn't stomach the thought of his lips on mine and bit him. "Bitch!" he shouted. He swung the gun and clocked me upside the head. Pain exploded behind my eyes. Stars floated in front of me. I tried to push him away, but he slapped me across the face so hard my teeth sliced into my cheek.

I cried out in pain.

"Stop!"

There was a commotion outside the door. I scooted away from Austin, hoping to use the distraction to make my escape. I knew without a doubt he was going to kill me if I didn't get away.

"Get away from her!" I heard Piper scream. At first, I thought it was in my head.

Austin was jerked away and tossed to the floor like a ragdoll. "Get her out of here," I heard Cooper shout.

I had to be dreaming. This couldn't be happening. I felt arms around me and fought. I didn't trust my brain. I was traumatized from captivity and probably suffering from some kind of brain injury.

"Tatum, it's me. It's Damon. I've got you. We have to get you out of here."

I heard Austin scream in pain. I focused my eyes on Cooper straddling him and punching the hell out of him. Austin's face was red with blood. Austin started fighting back. He clocked Cooper once, knocking his head back before bucking hard enough to throw Cooper off.

I screamed again. Austin couldn't get free. "Take her," Damon said.

Piper put her arm around my waist and started walking toward the door. I glanced over my shoulder and saw Damon hit Austin. The two of them took turns using Austin as a punching bag. "No!" I cried out.

Cooper stopped mid swing. "Get her out of here," he ordered.

"You're going to go down for this," Austin hissed and spat blood onto the floor.

"Really?" Cooper said as he grabbed Austin by the shirtfront and threw him against the wall. "I've got video evidence of you beating her and holding her prisoner. You are going to rot in hell for this."

"Let's go," Damon said and grabbed Cooper's arm before he could hit Austin again.

Cooper walked towards me, his eyes locked on mine. "Can you walk?"

"Yes, I'm fine."

"Let's go," Piper said. "This place gives me the creeps."

They led me out, passing two men lying unconscious in the hall. I assumed those were my guards. I had figured out Austin and the others didn't stay around when they weren't harassing me. Cooper helped me into his truck. Piper got into Damon's car and followed behind us.

I was afraid to speak. I was afraid to move. I didn't want to wake up and realize this wasn't real. My mind had been playing tricks on me. I would think I heard Cooper or wake up and think I was back in my own bed only to discover I was still a prisoner.

"Is this real?" I whispered.

Cooper reached over and gently squeezed my hand. "It's real."

Chapter Twenty-Four

Cooper

I PACED THE LIVING room. I was going to have to replace the floors with as much pacing had been done over the last four days.

"I should check on her," I said for the third time.

"Give her some time alone," Piper said from the kitchen.

"She needs to go to the hospital."

"Once she's out of the shower, we'll try and convince her," she replied calmly. "I've made her some tea. We'll get her to calm down and then we'll get her to the hospital."

Tatum came out of the bathroom with her wet hair hanging down her back. She was wearing a pair of yoga pants and one of my hoodies. There were dark circles under her eyes. Darker than I had ever seen before. A bruise was starting to show on the side of her face. Just the thought of that asshole hitting her made me want to beat the hell out of him once again.

"I've made you some tea," Piper said.

"Come sit down," I told her and helped her to the couch.

I watched as she sat down, wincing once. Piper handed her the tea, which she took a drink from. "Thank you."

"Baby, I know you said you were okay, but I would feel so much better if you would go to the hospital. We need to have your head checked out."

"I'm okay. He dazed me, but he didn't knock me out. I'm fine."

I stared at the cut on her cheek that had started to heal. I was afraid to ask how many other injuries she suffered. I wasn't sure I could handle it. "Are you hungry?"

She shook her head. "Not right now."

There was a brief silence. "Do you want to tell us what happened?"

She offered a small smile. "Honestly, not a lot. I was alone in that room for a long time. Actually, how long have I been gone?"

"Four days. Four fucking days that piece of shit kept you there."

"It wasn't just him. Gary and Wendy were in on it as well. Wendy is a fucking psychopath, by the way. How did you find me?"

I quickly filled her in on what we had learned over the last few days. "What video do you have?" she asked. "Do you really have proof?"

I smiled and patted my hat. I took it off and removed the small camera that we had mounted to the front of it. "I've got one too," Damon said.

"What do you have on the video?"

I shrugged. "We haven't watched it, but there is sure to be plenty to put his ass away. I need to call the detectives handling your case and let them know we found you. I can't wait to tell them I told them so. I knew Austin had a hand in this. They'll want to talk to you. I won't call them until you are ready for that."

"Thank you." She looked at Piper. "Did you meet with the lawyer?"

Piper shook her head. "No. I couldn't. I was a nervous wreck worrying about you."

Tatum groaned. "Great, they probably think I backed out of it."

Piper looked down at her hands. "I did try and reach out once yesterday. The secretary for the lawyer told me he wasn't interested in games and would be pursuing other options for his client."

Tatum cursed. "I know that's why Austin did this. He kept me from that meeting. They knew everything. Did you know they knew?"

"Alan told me he was being followed. These people aren't your average criminals. They have a large network and have been doing this for a while."

"We have to stop them," she said with a fierceness that belied her appearance.

"What do you want to do?" I asked her. I was willing to do anything she wanted as long as I was with her and could keep her safe.

"I need to talk to that author and make her understand I wasn't just yanking her chain. I need her to know this is real. She can't back down from this. She has to testify against Austin and provide proof she was the original author. My evidence means nothing if she doesn't want to pursue charges."

"Do you have her contact info?" Piper asked.

"On my computer, but I'd rather talk to her in person. I don't want her to have a way to ignore me. I want to look her in the eyes when I tell her I am not playing games."

"I can get you the information," I offered. "Alan has it all."

"Thank you. I'm going to change."

"You want to go now?" I asked with surprise.

"Yes. I need this done. The sooner we figure out what she wants to do, the sooner I get to get on with my life. I want Austin picked up, but I need Gary and Wendy arrested as well. They are the ones that are dangerous."

I was all for getting them all put away. "I'll call him."

I quickly made the call and got the information. Alan and his team were keeping an eye on the building. Austin had not left yet. That was a good thing. I wanted him at the scene of the crime when the cops showed up.

It was an hour later when we pulled up outside the address Alan gave me. The house was in a rough neighborhood and made me a little nervous. "You're sure you want to do this?" I asked her.

"Yes. Absolutely."

She marched right up the walkway and knocked on the door. A woman with a toddler on her hip opened the door. "Can I help you?"

"I'm Tatum. I spoke to you via email."

The woman rolled her eyes. "I don't have time for games. I know who you are and who you work for."

"I don't work for them," Tatum said.

"You've blown us off twice. You keep saying you have proof and you have yet to produce it."

Tatum held up her phone. "It's right here. I have a thumb drive I'll give you if you'll hear me out."

"Why should I trust you?"

"Because I've been kidnapped and held hostage the last four days because of what is on this recording."

The woman's eyes widened as she took a step back. "Oh."

"Can we come in?" I asked. I wasn't comfortable standing outside and being exposed.

"Yes, please do."

She put the toddler in a playpen. "Can I get you guys coffee? Water?"

"Coffee would be great," Tatum said with a smile.

My heart was so full of love for her. I was so damn grateful she was alive. We sat at the woman's dining table and drank cheap coffee from mismatched mugs. It was clear the woman was struggling financially. I now understood why Tatum was so insistent on making sure the woman got the money she was rightfully owed.

"So what's the proof?" she asked.

Tatum pulled up the recording that was stored on her phone. The woman listened with a slack jaw as Austin laughed about what he had done.

"Oh my goodness," she breathed. "I so want to take him down."

Tatum handed her the thumb drive. "Give that to your attorney. Maybe he can force them to settle. You deserve to get paid for your work."

"Thank you so much, and I'm sorry I thought you were a troll. After the first meeting, I wasn't sure you guys were real. Then my lawyer told me this was normal. The company was sending you in to find out what we had and what they could get away with offering."

"I'm sorry you had to go through this. Good luck to you. I will testify or sign a statement. Whatever you need."

"Thank you, and I hope you feel better."

Tatum smiled. "Thank you."

I nodded to the woman and escorted Tatum back to the truck. I kept my eyes open, looking for any sign we were being followed.

"Now where?" I asked her.

She blew out a breath. "I think it's time to go to the police and let them know I'm alive and found."

I grinned. "This is going to be good."

When I told the front desk officer my name and who I wanted to speak with, I didn't miss the look. I had been harassing the detectives for days. I wanted them to find her. I wasn't going to apologize for being desperate to get her back.

"Tatum Banks?" the detective asked with surprise when he stepped out front.

Tatum offered a smile. "That's me."

"Come with me," he said.

I wasn't about to leave her alone. I followed him into an interrogation room. Tatum told him her story. It was clear he was in a little disbelief. He looked at me, studying me close. "And you just waltzed into this criminal den and rescued her?"

I shrugged. "Basically."

"He's got it on video if you'd like to see," Tatum said innocently.

The detective almost choked. "No shit?"

"We thought you might want to see the proof of Austin's involvement."

The cop laughed. "We do enjoy a good video."

"Then you are going to love this."

He watched the footage, looking at me once when it came to the part that showed my fists hitting Austin. My face wasn't in the shot, which I was hoping would keep me from being charged with assault, but I really didn't care if I did get charged. I would take it.

"Sit tight for a minute," he said and left the room.

I looked at Tatum and gently touched the bruise. "How are you doing?"

"I'm good. I feel a lot better now."

"You're an amazing woman, Tatum. I still haven't fully processed the whole thing."

The detective came back in with two other men. "Can you please show them the video?"

Tatum replayed it. The three men exchanged a look before smiling at Tatum. "Can you forward that to me?" he asked and handed her a business card with his email.

"We put in a lot of man hours trying to find you," one of the new guys said. "It's nothing short of a miracle your boyfriend found you."

"I had a good PI. Weird, he had a handful of guys helping him and he found her."

"He was looking for one person. We're always looking for a hundred people."

I nodded. I still thought it was bullshit, but I had her back so I wasn't going to argue. "What happens now?" Tatum asked.

"We get a warrant for his arrest, and we go pick him up."

"What about Wendy and Gary?"

"We can get the owner of the building, but the other guy is going to be a little tougher to tie to this kidnapping."

"But I told you he was there," Tatum said.

"Yes, but it's your word against his. Don't worry, we'll get him. We'll get the first two and one of them will flip on him."

He sounded confident, but I wasn't quite as confident in his ability to keep her safe. "When?" I asked.

"I'd like to say we'll have them all rounded up by the end of the day, but there is a good chance they'll run. We'll get a car on the building just in case they try to run before we get the warrant."

"But you'll get them?" Tatum asked. "You aren't going to let them get away with this?"

The cop looked very serious. "I'm going to be honest with you, young lady. Your ex, Austin, he's screwed. I don't see him getting out, but the other suspect, Wendy, I don't have much to hold her on. If she lawyers up, she'll be out while she awaits trial."

Tatum's face paled. "And Gary?"

"Like I said, we need Wendy or Austin to tell us he was there."

"He gets away with it," she breathed.

"We're going to work on this," he assured her. "I would suggest she not be alone until we get everyone picked up."

"Not a chance," I told him.

We left the police station and went back to my house. Piper and Damon were still waiting for us. After we gave them the rundown of events, they left, and I tucked Tatum into bed with me holding her close. I didn't think I was ever going to let her go.

Chapter Twenty-Five

Tatum

I WOKE UP TO THE SOUND of a phone ringing. I heard Cooper's low voice beyond the bedroom door. I rubbed my eyes and looked over at the clock to see what time it was. "No way," I whispered.

The clock said it was after noon. I couldn't believe that, but the sun trying to peek through the heavy curtains on the bedroom window confirmed what I was reading on the clock. I couldn't believe I had slept so late. I rolled out of bed and went to find Cooper.

"Hi," I said.

He turned around and immediately came to me. He pulled me into his arms and held me. "Hi," he finally said and released me.

"You're not at work?"

"Not today."

"You don't have to stay with me," I told him.

"I want to."

"I'm glad you are here, though. I think I slept for sixteen hours!"

"You needed it. You can sleep all day if you want. I've got a grocery delivery coming in an hour. I'll make you some soup, and you can lie around."

"You're very sweet. Thank you for taking care of me."

"I will take care of you all day, every day."

"Thanks."

"That was the detective on the phone," he said.

My stomach dropped. Yesterday they had not been able to find him. He was on the run. The detective very plainly told me I was in danger and needed to be careful. I would have been terrified, but I had Cooper. I knew he would take care of me.

"And?"

He grinned. "They got him."

My shoulders sagged, and the breath left my lungs. "Thank goodness."

"They caught him trying to sneak into his penthouse. He was wearing some cheesy disguise. Apparently, he had money stashed in the apartment and wanted to get it so he could leave the state."

"I'm glad they got him, but Cooper, he isn't the mastermind behind this. It's Wendy and Gary."

"They got her as well."

I clapped my hands together. "They did?"

He nodded. "Yep. She was caught trying to board a plane to Mexico."

"Gary?"

"Not yet. Remember they have to get one of them to turn on him. Trust them to use their interrogation tactics."

"I'm glad they got them. I hope they never get out."

"Me too."

"I know it's late, but I need coffee."

"I'll make you some. Have a seat."

"Thank you."

I moved to stand in front of the window and stared out. It was a beautiful day. I was so glad I could actually see the sun. My time in captivity had deprived me of the simple gift of seeing the sun. I would never take the sun for granted again. Cooper moved up behind me, wrapping his arms around my waist and resting his chin on my head.

"Damon and Piper are on standby to bring over the rest of your things. You don't need to go back to the apartment."

"I'm fine. I can do it."

"Are you sure? Everything is already packed."

"I need to see it and then close that door for good."

"Okay, I get it."

When we got to my apartment, I was surprised by my reaction to seeing it again. I slowly walked upstairs. Piper and Damon were inside and doing the last bit of cleaning. I stood in the doorway and looked toward the kitchen. I replayed the moment the men had burst through the door.

"It's a good thing I'm moving," I said. "I don't think I could ever stay here again."

"Let's load that truck and get out of here," Piper said. "I'm creeped out being here."

It only took us an hour to load up Damon's car and Cooper's truck. My life had changed so much in the last few weeks. I would have never guessed I could go from where I was before to where I was now. Life was a whirlwind.

It was two days after my rescue, and I was beginning to feel normal. A new normal that included Cooper doting on me. I looked up from my spot in the corner of the gym. I had done a workout and was now working on Piper's book. Neither Cooper nor I was quite ready for me to be alone. He needed to work, which meant I became his shadow.

"Ready to get out of here?" Cooper asked.

I looked up from the laptop. "What time is it?"

"Four."

"Wow, the day flew by."

He grinned and kissed my forehead. "You've been pretty serious about that laptop."

"Her book is really good. I love it. I have to keep going back and rereading it because I get caught up in the story and forget I'm supposed to be editing."

He laughed as he took my hand. "We've got an hour to get home and get to the restaurant."

"This is the last double date," I told him. "Piper is on her own after this. If she still can't stand to be alone with Vance, she needs to cut him loose."

"I agree. Besides, I really want to spend some alone time with you."

"An hour huh?" I said as we got into his truck.

"Yep. I'll get a quick shower and change."

"I am feeling a little sticky myself," I said as we walked into the house. "Maybe I should take a shower."

He grinned as he pulled me into the bedroom. "I like the sound of that."

We stripped and stepped into the shower he had just recently updated. "I love you," I told him and looked up at him. "I'm so glad to be alive."

"I love you."

He kissed me with water sluicing down my face and shoulders. It was the first time we'd had sex since I'd been rescued. I needed him. I needed his physical strength. His hands slid down my body before he slowly turned me to face the wall. His back blocked the spray of the shower as he kissed down the back of my neck.

"I've missed you," he breathed.

"I was so worried I wouldn't get to do this with you ever again. I was staring death in the face, and all I could think about was sex."

He chuckled before running his tongue across my shoulder. His hand slipped between my legs. I opened my legs wider and slightly bent forward. His fingers parted my folds, making way for him to enter me. He slipped inside, gently pushing himself deep. His arm wrapped around my waist and anchored me to him.

"I don't think I could have gone on without you. I couldn't live without this."

He began to move, sliding in and out of me and teasing me into a frenzy. When the orgasm hit, we were both overcome with emotion. The release was exactly what I needed to feel like my life was going to be normal again. I was alive and well, and I had the best man in the world by my side.

"We should probably get a move on," he whispered against my ear.

I groaned. "Can't we just tell her we need a raincheck?"

"I'm down for it, but she might not be very happy with you. I promise we'll keep dinner short, and we'll have dessert at home."

I turned in his arms and held his face in my hands. "I like the sound of that."

When we got to the restaurant, we were about fifteen minutes late. Piper shot me a glare as we sat down. "Sorry, we got held up," I said.

"How are you doing?" Vance asked.

"I'm getting back into the groove of things," I told him.

"I'm glad you are okay."

"Thank you."

"So Piper was just filling me in on the whole story. She said you are some kind of hero."

I laughed, feeling myself blush a little. "Cooper and Piper are the heroes. They saved me."

"And now I can officially date Piper," he said with a laugh. "She's put me through my paces."

Piper smiled at him. "I had to see if you were serious."

"And she can't use me as an excuse anymore," I added.

"Nope, she can't, and I won't let her."

We enjoyed a great meal and even better conversation. Piper was happy. I hoped she could let down her guard and enjoy the man. He seemed honest and reliable. He would be good for her. We wished them a good night and made our excuses to leave the moment the ticket hit the table.

Chapter Twenty-Six

Cooper

WAKING UP WITH HER in my arms was the best thing in the world. I had come to cherish these moments early in the morning when she was still asleep. I listened to her breathing and inhaled the scent of her hair. These were moments I would never take for granted. I had almost lost her. I almost never got the chance to wake up with her in my arms.

We'd been through hell and were finally coming out on the other side. It was hard not to hate Austin, but hating him didn't help anything. I was trying to forget about him. I didn't want to give him the energy it took to hate him. He was out of her life. Out of my life. His fate was yet to be determined, but I had no doubt he was going to prison for a while.

"Is it morning?" she murmured.

"It is."

She snuggled closer to me. "I am so glad I get to wake up with you just like this every morning."

"I kind of like it myself."

She pinched my nipple. "You kind of like it?"

I laughed and pushed her hand away. "I love it. I wouldn't have it any other way."

She raised her face to mine. Her bruise was gone, and she was my old Tatum once again. "I love living here with you."

"Me too."

"You're not tired of me yet?" she teased.

"Not yet. Ask me again in a week."

She pinched my nipple again. "You are feeling mighty feisty this morning."

"Yes I am," I growled and pulled her over me.

She bent down and kissed me before jumping off me and taking most of the blankets with her.

"Where are you going?" I complained.

"I'm going to make coffee and breakfast. Today is a new day. I'm ready to take back control. I'm ready to find a job and start living again."

"You know you don't need to rush right out and do that," I told her. "Take some time."

She was already out of the bedroom. "I've taken a week. I'm not taking another day."

I followed her into the kitchen. "Are you sure? Like you said, it's only been a week. You don't need to worry about paying anything here."

"I have my own bills, and I'm not going to be a mooch. I can pay. I need to pay. If I stay inside and stop living my life because of what they did, they win. They get to have all the power. I'm not letting them beat me."

I smiled and nodded. "All right. I get it. If you're ready, then I think it's a great idea."

"I am ready. Shower, and I'll make your usual eggs and toast."

I gave her a kiss. "Thank you, baby. You know you don't have to make me breakfast every day?"

"I do know that, but I like to. Besides, it's the least I can do for my sugar daddy."

I swatted her ass before walking back to the bedroom. I was happy. Like the kind of happy that could happen when the stars and moon aligned, and everything was just perfect. Having her in my life, in my home, it was amazing. It was so much better than I ever expected it could be. She'd changed me. She made me see everything more clearly. I knew what I wanted and was already planning to ask her to marry me. I wasn't ever leaving her, and I was going to make sure she didn't leave me. Austin was out of the way, and there was nothing that could get in the way of our happiness.

When I returned to the kitchen, she was just putting the plate of over-easy eggs on the table. I sat down and waited for her. "What's your schedule like today?" she asked.

I shrugged. "Not bad. I've got a new guy coming in. We'll see if we are a good fit."

"I'm sure you will be."

"What about you? Are you going to do some cold calls or look on-line?"

"Both. I want to turn my resume in to a few of the publishing houses in person. I'm hoping they will love me and give me an interview on the spot. I've made a couple of calls but so far nothing. I'm sure it has something to do with Austin and Gary's blackmail. It's going to take a while to rid my reputation of that stain."

Her phone beeped. She reached for it and read the message. "Oh no," she groaned. "It's from Piper. I'll send you the link."

I grabbed my own phone and read the headlines. "You knew that was coming," I told her.

"I did, but I never really expected my kidnapping to be such big news. I'm just little old me."

"With the number of flyers we papered this city with, you are a hell of a lot more than little old you. Everyone knows who you are."

"Oh my gosh!" she exclaimed. "The publishing house is trending on Twitter."

"Good or bad?"

"Mostly bad. Oh, they put out an official statement."

"What does it say?" I was too busy reading an article about her kidnapping and the heroic effort of the police department to save her. I didn't mind that they got the credit. They could have it. I had her, and that was far more important.

She cleared her throat. "We are deeply saddened to hear about the traumatic events surrounding our former employee, Tatum Banks. The actions of Wendy Kirpatrick and Austin Scott do not represent who we are as a company. We value our employees and are actively looking into the situation. The rumors of plagiarism are equally devastating. We have helped new, young authors launch their first works for more than twenty years. We pride ourselves in helping our authors take their visions and turn them into reality. Our fraud team is opening an investigation into the claims of plagiarism. Our heart goes out to Tatum, and we hope she recovers quickly."

I snorted and shook my head. "Gee, really?"

"No shit. If they actually cared and wanted to support me, they could give me my job back."

"Do you want your job back?" I asked.

"No, but I don't want the fired thing on my resume. They never did mention why I no longer worked there. I could so sue their asses."

"You could, but do you want to keep dragging this thing out?"

"No, I don't. I want it over and to put it behind me. But if I can't get a job because of this bullshit, I will go after them. I will demand they write me a recommendation letter. They owe me that much."

"They owe you a lot more than that."

"No mention of Gary?"

"Nope."

I sipped my coffee. "Do you think they know about his involvement?"

She smiled and leaned forward. "If they don't yet, they will. Once the lawyers for those authors file suit and the evidence is laid out, everyone is going to know."

"He deserves to have his shit blasted all over the damn internet. Everyone needs to know what kind of man he is. He's worse than a fucking mob boss."

"I agree. What about your hot housewife? Has she ever shown up?"

I shook my head. "Not a peep. I'll revoke her membership to the gym. I don't want her near me."

"She might not have known what her husband was doing," she said.

"I don't believe that for a second. She knows. It's why she was afraid of him. She had me meet him because she was worried he would do something. She clearly knows what kind of man he is. I don't want any association with her or her husband. I don't care if she's innocent. I don't want the connection."

"I understand, and I appreciate your loyalty."

"I will absolutely always be loyal to you and you alone."

"How long do you think it will take for the shit to hit the fan?" she asked.

"Not a clue."

She was quiet for several seconds. "Do you think I'll be in danger once his role in the scheme comes out?"

It was something that had been weighing heavily on me. "I do. I know you said you didn't want it before, but I think it would be a good idea to have Alan keep an eye on things when the real story breaks. He'll be completely unobtrusive. I am not trying to take your freedom, and if you say no, I will respect your decision."

She smiled. "Alan saved my life. Yes, I will agree to have him follow me around *if* the story gets out and *if* it looks like Gary might come after me."

That was a huge relief. "Thank you."

"How is he, by the way? The detective didn't seem too happy when he was here the other day."

I laughed. "The detective can be as unhappy as he wants. Alan did his job, and he did it better than the public servant. He knows what to say to stay out of jail. They can't prove he broke the law."

"I'm so grateful he did what he did. I can't imagine what would have happened to me if he hadn't broken the law. Two minutes later—"

She didn't have to finish the sentence. We both knew what would have happened if it had been two minutes later. Austin was ready to kill her, and he didn't appear to be all that bothered about doing it.

"But I was there. We were there. You're here and you're safe."

"I know."

"You aren't going out alone today, are you?"

"Piper will be with me. Vance too."

That gave me some relief. Vance wasn't a small guy, and he'd put up a fight if someone tried to snatch her again. "Good. You'll check in with me throughout the day?"

"Yes. I know you're worried, but I can't live my life in fear. I have to pick up where I left off. He's not going to win."

"I know. I get it, and I will support you. I just wish I could be there to guard your sexy ass."

She winked. "This sexy ass will be waiting for you when you get home."

Chapter Twenty-Seven

Tatum

THE CAB DROPPED ME off in the center of the business district where I was meeting Piper. Vance had been unable to come, but I was not telling Cooper that until I got home tonight. I didn't want him to worry or insist on taking yet another day off to babysit me.

"Tatum!" I heard Piper call out.

I walked to where she was sitting on a bench with dark sunglasses on. "You look very mysterious." She smiled and lifted her glasses. I cringed when I saw the dark circles under her eyes. "Damn, what happened to you?"

She pulled the glasses back on. "Vance. That man is a machine. I think I only got two hours of sleep last night."

I burst into laughter. "You finally took him to bed! It's about damn time. You have far more self-control than I do."

"I wanted to make sure it was real. I didn't want him chasing me because of my connection to the internet superstar of the month."

"Didn't you meet him before all my drama happened?"

"Yes, but still. You never know. People are crazy."

I snorted, thinking about Wendy. "Don't I know it."

"He is really a great guy," she said with a sigh. "I like him."

"Duh, he likes you as well. You are damn lucky he didn't dump your ass for playing so hard to get."

"Trust me, I made up for it last night."

"Good for you."

"How's it going with you? Are you settled in? Ready to get your own place yet?"

"I love where I live. I love waking up with him and going to bed with him. I'm happy. Really, really happy."

"I'm happy for you. How is he taking the whole internet story this morning?"

"He's worried Gary might try to come after me. If Gary's involvement is revealed, I've agreed to let Alan be my bodyguard of sorts."

"Good. That makes me feel better."

"Let's go," I said and got up from the bench. "I need to start pounding the pavement. I can't let Cooper support me. I need a job."

"Why don't you take some time off?"

I rolled my eyes. "Now you sound like him. I need to work. I'm not independently wealthy, and I happen to like working. I want a job."

"I get that, but you could play the little housewife to Cooper for a while."

I shook my head. "Nope. I'm getting a job. I don't care if I'm the assistant to the assistant editor. I'm getting my foot back in the door."

She sighed and got up. "I tried."

"Yes, you did. Now we'll start over here."

We spent the next three hours essentially knocking on doors. I was rejected at almost every turn. I wasn't giving up. It had been a struggle to get the first editing job. Perseverance would pay off. It was just day one of my search.

"Let's go back to my place," Piper said after we enjoyed a very late lunch.

I checked the time. "Okay. Cooper still has a couple of hours left at the gym."

We caught an Uber to her place and opened a bottle of wine. I was sure the invitation was more of a request. No one wanted me to be alone. I knew it was because they loved me and were worried about me. I couldn't be upset they were trying to take care of me. It was very sweet, and I appreciated their attentiveness.

"How's the book going?" I asked her.

"I thought it was done, and then an idea came to me in the middle of the night and I found myself reopening the thing."

"Really? You are really rolling on this one."

"I know. I love it. I finally feel like I've found my stride. I've already got three more books cooking in the back of my head. I'm excited to work. The first couple of books felt strained. I basically had to force myself to finish them. This one, I don't want it to end. It's going to end up being nine hundred pages."

I laughed. "As your editor, I have to advise against that."

"Yes, Miss Editor."

"I'm about halfway through what you've sent me," I told her. "I'm sorry it's taking so long. Between Cooper hovering and answering questions from the police, I have had very little time, which is crazy considering I'm jobless."

"Take your time. I'm not done with it, and like I said before, I want to drag my feet. My lawyer is certain he found a way out of my contract. They could still demand a portion of the profits from this one, but I don't care. If it allows me to keep the book out of their hands, I'll give them half. I want nothing to do with them."

"Oh, did you see, they dropped two authors this morning!"

She nodded. "I did. I'm guessing they can't control them. This whole stolen book thing is about to blow up. They are trying to limit the damage."

"You know, I hate to say this, but when this comes out, there is a good chance you are going to suffer some major blowback. When it's revealed the bulk of their catalog is plagiarized work, people are going to question the authenticity of your books."

"I know. My lawyer is drafting a statement and wants me to provide him with my rough drafts in case we have to prove it was really my work."

I grimaced. "I'm sorry you are getting dragged into this."

"It isn't your fault. I wish I would have researched the company a little better before I signed with them. I was just so excited to actually get a deal, I jumped without looking."

"That's what they counted on. They went after young authors who didn't have a team to advise them. It's scandalous, and I cannot wait for Gary to go down for what he's done."

"I feel a little bad for the authors that are going down with him."

I finished my glass of wine. "Not me. They knew damn well what they were doing was wrong. They knew they didn't write those books, but they went along with it. They are complicit."

"Damn, you are harsh."

"I've been kidnapped, beaten, and fired. I'm a little bitter."

She laughed. "I guess you get a pass on that."

I checked the time and saw a message from Cooper. I quickly texted him and let him know I was okay and with Piper. "I should probably get going. I want to be home when Cooper gets there." I ordered a ride, anxious to get home.

"Ah, you are the little woman."

"Maybe a little. It's kind of fun cooking for him. I feel so domesticated."

"You better watch out; you're going to find yourself barefoot and pregnant in his kitchen."

I grinned. "Only if I'm lucky."

My phone beeped. It was Cooper with a naughty message. I smiled and sent him an equally naughty one back.

"He knows you're with me, right?"

"Yes, he's just worried. I'm sure once all of this is behind us, he won't need me to check in all the time."

"Gee, why would he be worried? You're with me. We're a kickass team."

We both laughed. The last time we hung out together we both ended up knocked out. "What could possibly go wrong?" I joked.

"I have pepper spray now," she said. "And a bat."

"Um, don't you remember how fast it happened?" I asked her. "Cooper has demanded I keep pepper spray as well, but I just don't know how I'm supposed to get it out of my purse and spray an attacker before they disable me."

"We should take self-defense classes," she said.

"That is an excellent idea! I bet Cooper knows someone. I'll ask him tonight."

"I want to be able to kick ass," she said excitedly.

"You did a damn good job of kicking ass when it happened. You were like a wildcat. If I wasn't in shock, I probably could have helped you instead of standing there like a dumbass and watching you scratch and claw."

She laughed and held out her hands. "My nails were short before, but after that night, they were down below the skin."

"Ouch," I said. I never really knew how much she'd suffered. She'd been almost healed by the time I was rescued. "I don't know if I've said it, but thank you for what you did that night. You gave it your all. Thank you for that."

"I just wish I had more to give. I wish I could have prevented it altogether."

"We can't dwell on it," I said and shook off the negative feelings. "We are pushing on."

"Yes, we are."

"Thanks for hanging with me today. I'll call you tomorrow."

"Text me when you get home."

I sighed but nodded. "I will."

I waited on the curb for the Uber to show up. A car pulled up and I quickly got in the backseat. I pulled on my seatbelt and glanced out the window.

"Thank you," the driver said as he pulled away from the curb.

I glanced at the back of his head. It was the first time I had been thanked for getting in a car. "You're welcome."

"I am glad we are going to do this the easy way," the man said.

Something registered, and I suddenly felt a shiver of dread roll down my spine. "Excuse me?" I said and reached for the door handle.

Gary turned around and smiled. "You and I need to have a little chat."

I felt the blood rush from my face. I tried the door handle. Nothing happened. His laughter floated around me. This was the moment my life flashed before my eyes.

THE END

Perfect Revenge

Karma Series

Walk Away
Make Him Pay
Perfect Revenge

Find Lexy Timms:

LEXY TIMMS NEWSLETTER:
http://eepurl.com/9i0vD
Lexy Timms Facebook Page:
https://www.facebook.com/SavingForever
Lexy Timms Website:
http://www.lexytimms.com

Want

FREE READS?

Sign up for Lexy Timms' newsletter
And she'll send you updates on new releases,
ARC copies of books and a whole lotta fun!

Sign up for news and updates!
http://eepurl.com/9i0vD

More by Lexy Timms:

FROM BEST SELLING AUTHOR, Lexy Timms, comes a billionaire romance that'll make you swoon and fall in love all over again.

Jamie Connors has given up on men. Despite being smart, pretty, and just slightly overweight, she's a magnet for the kind of guys that don't stay around.

Her sister's wedding is at the foreground of the family's attention. Jamie would be fine with it if her sister wasn't pressuring her to lose weight so she'll fit in the maid of honor dress, her mother would get off her case and her ex-boyfriend wasn't about to become her brother-in-law.

Determined to step out on her own, she accepts a PA position from billionaire Alex Reid. The job includes an apartment on his property and gets her out of living in her parent's basement.

Jamie must balance her life and somehow figure out how to manage her billionaire boss, without falling in love with him.

** The Boss is book 1 in the Managing the Bosses series. All your questions won't be answered in the first book. It may end on a cliff hanger.

For mature audiences only. There are adult situations, but this is a love story, NOT erotica.

Managing the Billionaire Series

Never Enough

Worth the Cost

Secret Admirers

Chasing Affection

Pressing Romance

Timeless Memories

Darkest Night Series

Savage

Vicious

Brutal

Sinful

Fierce

Faking It Description:

HE GROANED. THIS WAS torture. Being trapped in a room with a beautiful woman was just about every man's fantasy, but he had to remember that this was just pretend.

Allyson Smith has crushed on her boss for years, but never dared to make a move. When she finds herself without a date to her brother's upcoming wedding, Allyson tells her family one innocent white lie: that she's been dating her boss. Unfortunately, her boss discovers her lie, and insists on posing as her boyfriend to escort her to the wedding.

Playboy billionaire Dane Prescott always has a new heiress on his arm, but he can't get his assistant Allyson out of his head. He's fought his attraction to her, until he gets caught up in her scheme of a fake relationship.

One passionate weekend with the boss has Allyson Smith questioning everything she believes in. Falling for a wealthy playboy like Dane is against the rules, but if she's just faking it what's the harm?

THE ONE YOU CAN'T FORGET

Emily Rose Dougherty is a good Catholic girl from mythical Walkerville, CT. She had somehow managed to get herself into a heap trouble with the law, all because an ex-boyfriend has decided to make things difficult.

Luke "Spade" Wade owns a Motorcycle repair shop and is the Road Captain for Hades' Spawn MC. He's shocked when he reads in the paper that his old high school flame has been arrested. She's always been the one he couldn't forget.

Will destiny let them find each other again? Or what happens in the past, best left for the history books?

*** This is book 1 of the Hades' Spawn MC Series. All your questions may not be answered in the first book.*

FORTUNE RIDERS INC.
BILLIONAIRE BIKER
LEXY TIMMS
Download For
FREE
Lexy
Timms

Don't miss out!

Visit the website below and you can sign up to receive emails whenever Lexy Timms publishes a new book. There's no charge and no obligation.

https://books2read.com/r/B-A-NNL-WPPMB

Did you love *Make Him Pay*? Then you should read *Building Billions - Part 1*[1] by Lexy Timms!

By *USA Today Bestselling Author, Lexy Timms.*

One night love affair

It was only supposed to be one night. Ashley's just a low step on the ladder of her company's success. The company party was always a big to-do. Jimmy Sheldon, the CEO and found of Big Steps always made sure his employees had a good time. He should, he worked them hard, expected more than they thought they could give, but he always rewarded their efforts. It's what made him a great boss and the owner of a million-dollar company. He knew how to make things work.

And boy, did he.

---

1. https://books2read.com/u/mVZy02

2. https://books2read.com/u/mVZy02

A few too many cosmo's and Ashley hit the dance floor. She forgot how much fun it was to dance. After a few songs, her years of competitive dance routines came back to her and she had everyone trying to move like her. Even boss-man Jimmy. And he had some decent dance moves himself.

From the dance floor to the hotel room, Ashley swore they'd both forget what happened in the morning and go back to their steps on the ladder.

Except, no one ever forgets a hit song...

Building Billions:

Part 1

Part 2

Part 3

Read more at www.lexytimms.com.

Also by Lexy Timms

A Bad Boy Bullied Romance
I Hate You
I Hate You A Little Bit
I Hate You A Little Bit More

A Burning Love Series
Spark of Passion
Flame of Desire
Blaze of Ecstasy

A Chance at Forever Series
Forever Perfect
Forever Desired
Forever Together

A Dating App Series
I've Been Matched
You've Been Matched

We've Been Matched

A "Kind of" Billionaire
Taking a Risk
Safety in Numbers
Pretend You're Mine

A Maybe Series
Maybe I Should
Maybe I Shouldn't
Maybe I Did

Assisting the Boss Series
Billion Reasons
Duke of Delegation
Late Night Meetings
Delegating Love
Suitors and Admirers

BBW Romance Series
Capturing Her Beauty
Pursuing Her Dreams
Tracing Her Curves

Beating the Biker Series

Making Her His
Making the Break
Making of Them

Betrayal at the Bay Series
Devil's Bay
Devil's Deceit

Billionaire Banker Series
Banking on Him
Price of Passion
Investing in Love
Knowing Your Worth
Treasured Forever
Banking on Christmas
Billionaire Banker Box Set Books #1-3

Billionaire CEO Brothers
Tempting the Player
Late Night Boardroom
Reviewing the Perfomance
Result of Passion
Directing the Next Move
Touching the Assets

Billionaire Holiday Romance Series

Driving Home for Christmas
The Valentine Getaway
Cruising Love
Billionaire Holiday Romance Box Set

Billionaire in Disguise Series
Facade
Illusion
Charade

Billionaire Secrets Series
The Secret
Freedom
Courage
Trust
Impulse
Billionaire Secrets Box Set Books #1-3

Blind Sight Series
See Me
Fix Me
Eyes On Me

Branded Series
Money or Nothing
What People Say

Give and Take

Building Billions
Building Billions - Part 1
Building Billions - Part 2
Building Billions - Part 3

Butler & Heiress Series
To Serve
For Duty
No Chore
All Wrapped Up

Change of Heart Series
The Heart Needs
The Heart Wants
The Heart Knows

Conquering Warrior Series
Ruthless

Counting the Billions
Counting the Days
Counting On You
Counting the Kisses

Cry Wolf Reverse Harem Series
Beautiful & Wild
Misunderstood
Never Tamed

Darkest Night Series
Savage
Vicious
Brutal
Sinful
Fierce

Diamond in the Rough Anthology
Billionaire Rock
Billionaire Rock - part 2

Dirty Little Taboo Series
Flirting Touch
Denying Pleasure
Forbidding Desire
Craving Passion

Dominating PA Series
Her Personal Assistant - Part 1

Her Personal Assistant - Part 2
Her Personal Assistant Box Set

Fake Billionaire Series
Faking It
Temporary CEO
Caught in the Act
Never Tell A Lie
Fake Christmas
Fake Billionaire Box Set #1-3

Firehouse Romance Series
Caught in Flames
Burning With Desire
Craving the Heat
Firehouse Romance Complete Collection

Forging Billions Series
Dirty Money
Petty Cash
Payment Required

For His Pleasure
Elizabeth
Georgia
Madison

Fortune Riders MC Series
Billionaire Biker
Billionaire Ransom
Billionaire Misery
Fortune Riders Box Set - Books #1-3

Fragile Series
Fragile Touch
Fragile Kiss
Fragile Love

Great Temptation Series
The Devil's Footsteps
Heaven's Command
Mortals Surrender

Hades' Spawn Motorcycle Club
One You Can't Forget
One That Got Away
One That Came Back
One You Never Leave
One Christmas Night
Hades' Spawn MC Complete Series

Hard Rocked Series
Rhyme
Harmony
Lyrics

Heart of Stone Series
The Protector
The Guardian
The Warrior

Heart of the Battle Series
Celtic Viking
Celtic Rune
Celtic Mann
Heart of the Battle Series Box Set

Heistdom Series
Master Thief
Goldmine
Diamond Heist
Smile For Me
Your Move
Green With Envy
Saving Money

Chasing Justice
Pursuing Justice
Justice - Complete Series

Karma Series
Walk Away
Make Him Pay

Kissed by Billions
Kissed by Passion
Kissed by Desire
Kissed by Love

Leaning Towards Trouble
Trouble
Discord
Tenacity

Love on the Sea Series
Ships Ahoy
Rough Sea
High Tide

Love You Series
Love Life

Need Love
My Love

Managing the Billionaire
Never Enough
Worth the Cost
Secret Admirers
Chasing Affection
Pressing Romance
Timeless Memories
Managing the Billionaire Box Set Books #1-3

Managing the Bosses Series
The Boss
The Boss Too
Who's the Boss Now
Love the Boss
I Do the Boss
Wife to the Boss
Employed by the Boss
Brother to the Boss
Senior Advisor to the Boss
Forever the Boss
Christmas With the Boss
Billionaire in Control
Billionaire Makes Millions
Billionaire at Work
Precious Little Thing
Priceless Love
Valentine Love

The Cost of Freedom
Trick or Treat
The Night Before Christmas
Gift for the Boss - Novella 3.5
Managing the Bosses Box Set #1-3
Managing the Bosses Novellas

Mislead by the Bad Boy Series
Deceived
Provoked
Betrayed

Model Mayhem Series
Shameless
Modesty
Imperfection

Moment in Time
Highlander's Bride
Victorian Bride
Modern Day Bride
A Royal Bride
Forever the Bride

Mountain Millionaire Series
Close to the Ridge

Crossing the Bluff
Climbing the Mount

My Best Friend's Sister
Hometown Calling
A Perfect Moment
Thrown in Together

My Darker Side Series
Darkest Hour
Time to Stop
Against the Light

Neverending Dream Series
Neverending Dream - Part 1
Neverending Dream - Part 2
Neverending Dream - Part 3
Neverending Dream - Part 4
Neverending Dream - Part 5

Outside the Octagon
Submit
Fight
Knockout

Protecting Diana Series
Her Bodyguard
Her Defender
Her Champion
Her Protector
Her Forever

Protecting Layla Series
His Mission
His Objective
His Devotion

Racing Hearts Series
Rush
Pace
Fast

Regency Romance Series
The Duchess Scandal - Part 1
The Duchess Scandal - Part 2

Reverse Harem Series
Primals
Archaic

Unitary

RIP Series
Track the Ripper
Hunt the Ripper
Pursue the Ripper

R&S Rich and Single Series
Alex Reid
Parker
Sebastian

Saving Forever
Saving Forever - Part 1
Saving Forever - Part 2
Saving Forever - Part 3
Saving Forever - Part 4
Saving Forever - Part 5
Saving Forever - Part 6
Saving Forever Part 7
Saving Forever - Part 8
Saving Forever Boxset Books #1-3

Secrets & Lies Series
Strange Secrets
Evading Secrets

Inspiring Secrets
Lies and Secrets
Mastering Secrets
Alluring Secrets
Secrets & Lies Box Set Books #1-3

Shifting Desires Series
Jungle Heat
Jungle Fever
Jungle Blaze

Sin Series
Payment for Sin
Atonement Within
Declaration of Love

Southern Romance Series
Little Love Affair
Siege of the Heart
Freedom Forever
Soldier's Fortune

Spanked Series
Passion
Playmate
Pleasure

Extra! Extra!
Read All About It
Stop the Press
Breaking News
This Just In
The Golden Mail Box Set Books #1-3

The Lucky Billionaire Series
Lucky Break
Streak of Luck
Lucky in Love

The Sound of Breaking Hearts Series
Disruption
Destroy
Devoted

The University of Gatica Series
The Recruiting Trip
Faster
Higher
Stronger
Dominate
No Rush
University of Gatica - The Complete Series

Unlucky Series
Unlucky in Love
UnWanted
UnLoved Forever

War Torn Letters Series
My Sweetheart
My Darling
My Beloved

Wet & Wild Series
Stormy Love
Savage Love
Secure Love

Worth It Series
Worth Billions
Worth Every Cent
Worth More Than Money

You & Me - A Bad Boy Romance
Just Me
Touch Me
Kiss Me

Watch for more at www.lexytimms.com.

About the Author

"Love should be something that lasts forever, not is lost forever." Visit USA TODAY BESTSELLING AUTHOR, LEXY TIMMS https://www.facebook.com/SavingForever *Please feel free to connect with me and share your comments. I love connecting with my readers.* Sign up for news and updates and freebies - I like spoiling my readers! http://eepurl.com/9i0vD website: www.lexytimms.com Dealing in Antique Jewelry and hanging out with her awesome hubby and three kids, Lexy Timms loves writing in her free time. MANAGING THE BOSSES is a bestselling 10-part series dipping into the lives of Alex Reid and Jamie Connors. Can a secretary really fall for her billionaire boss?

Read more at www.lexytimms.com.

www.ingramcontent.com/pod-product-compliance
Lightning Source LLC
Chambersburg PA
CBHW051952150726
47999CB00004B/1351